HIS VAMPIRE PRINCESS

A DARK VINTAGE NOVELLA

INES JOHNSON

Published in the United States of America

Special Edition: April 2025

Page edges by Painted Wings Publishing Services

This book is a work of fiction. While reference might be made to actual historical events or existing locations, the names, characters, places and incidents are either the product of the authors' imaginations or are used fictitiously, and any resemblance to actual persons, living or dead, business establishments, events, or locales is entirely coincidental.

1

Arneis

"The reports are in, Councilman Durand," says my policy advisor. "They're not good."

I clench my fists as I sit back at my desk. The piece of furniture is small and made of cheap wood. There is a series of chips around the edges that have caused snags on my expensive suits one too many times. Grooves of graphite from my predecessors who wanted to leave their mark on this city and its community can be found in the drawers. I tighten my hold around the pen in my hand, wondering if I should do the same thing. Because it might not be my desk for much longer.

"You've slipped in the polls."

Polling for local elections was laughable. Less than twenty percent of any given city, town, or municipality came out to vote for the seats of mayors, council members, or board members. Though I serve a diverse constituency of coeds and soccer moms, indigenous peoples and rednecks, scholars, and prostitutes, very few of them know my name or what I've done for them.

I funneled more money over into the education budget that allowed each child in Tucson to have a computer in the classroom. I filled every reported pothole over the last two years. I lowered the residents' taxes and balanced the budget, putting the city in the black.

The city hasn't seen this kind of economic boom in years, maybe even decades. But I'm about to lose my place in this worn seat and crumbling desk, all because of a photo. A reporter had captured a shot of me walking out of an underground sex club late one night a few weeks ago.

"We just need to highlight your good work; remind the people why they voted for you four years ago."

They voted for me because of my family name. The Durand Vineyard is a generations-old establishment in Arizona, and I'm its prince. I've lived all twenty-five years of my life on a strait-laced path, much like the rows of grapes on my family's land. I had been groomed to take over from my father and run the business alongside my two sisters. But on my first day of high school, I happened into the school library and stumbled upon a student government meeting.

Seeing Robert's Rules of Order at work had fascinated my mind. I was used to straight rows of vines, predictable harvest times, and the precise measurements of wine blends. I liked things old, orderly, and results-oriented. By the following year, I was the class vice president. Every year that followed, I was elected president.

Before this scandal, I was on the trajectory to become city mayor. I had my sights set on congressman. But even though the story only ran on the second page of the local rag, my future is now blurred. Likely less than ten percent of my constituency read the papers, but it is enough to potentially lose my seat. All because of a photograph that's been taken out of context.

"Perhaps a new video ad where we show the people your clean-cut image to detract from—"

My gaze shoots up. The young man before me squirms. He was an intern not long ago. I elevated him to this position when I saw his hunger as a political animal.

He thinks he's dealing with a man's base needs. I don't have those. I'm not a saint, but I'm as close to it as any modern man could get.

Despite what that gossip rag printed, I've never had group or public sex. I've never taken my clothes off outside of a locked bedroom with the lights off. I've only had sex with two women, and not at the same time. Charlotte Pratt and I waited three months before taking our relationship behind closed doors. With Amber Walt, who I'd thought would become Mrs. Councilman Durand, I waited six months into our committed relationship.

That photograph of me coming out of Club Toxic was not the whole picture. That salacious report of what I'd been doing inside is complete fiction. The problem is, the actual facts surrounding the story sound more like science fiction and fantasy than the voters would believe.

"Where are you going, sir?"

"To clear my name of this nonsense," I say as I

slide into my suit jacket and straighten my tie. Ever since my first election as class president, I've worn a suit and tie every day, except for on the weekends. Then I wear a collared shirt and pressed slacks to relax.

On the streets, the sun is starting to set. Masked goblins and witches roam from door to door. Super-heroes' capes trail behind as children run up to open doors to receive their rewards. I'd forgotten it was Halloween. I probably should've dismissed my staff to go home early, but like me, they are all worka-holics who live for the job.

Once in my car, I pull out of the city. Concrete buildings give way to rolling green pastures. The fields of green are spotted with the colorful heads of grapes. It's harvest time, and many workers are out tending to the crops that will make the older citizens celebrating this festive holiday drunk in just a matter of hours.

I drive past the turn that would take me to my family's vineyard. Memories flood my mind, of my time there with my family. My older sister Marechal, who was forever in the lab blending berries, but would always look up when I wanted to run a debate strategy past her. My baby sister Cari, who loved to color in my homemade campaign signs, insisting her color scheme would be my winning strategy.

I see both their smiling faces looking at me with trust and love. But as I wind along the road to my destination, my mind begins to fog. The curves of the lane bend. In my mind, things get dark and twisted and bloody.

Memory is a fickle thing. I remember the night I went into Club Toxic to seek out its owner, Lucius Frangelico. The billionaire was trying to purchase my family's vineyard out from under us. I walked into a nightclub on family business, and I left a sex dungeon as a sexual deviant.

The funniest part is that, during my business meeting, everyone inside the club had been fully clothed. The young people had been rubbing up against one another in the act of sexual desire. But no one's base needs were being totally satisfied on the dance floor. That had all been happening a floor below.

It wasn't widely known that there was any sexual activity going on in the club. I certainly hadn't known it the night I'd gone in. Nor when I'd come out. Which leads me to believe that Frangelico and his minions were behind my demise.

They've taken my family's business. They've

taken both of my sisters. And now they are trying to take my career.

I park my car in front of the Serrano vineyard as the last rays of the sun set. I've been to this house a couple of times. One such instance, I have almost forgotten. Because the Serranos have taken my memories from me.

"Arneis? Is that you?" My sister Cari's voice comes from the other side of the door. "I can smell you from all the way inside, isn't that crazy? But don't worry, I already ate tonight."

"Cari, that's not funny," says Marechal as she opens the great doors.

I stand on the other side of the threshold, gaping down at my sisters. They look exactly the same, but I know they are different. Like me, they both sport bite marks on their necks.

About a month ago, my baby sister got herself in a relationship with a dead man walking. That isn't hyperbole. Hadrian Serrano is a vampire. And just a few days ago, my older sister Marechal got in bed with Serrano's brother, Gaius. I'm convinced both of the creatures mind-wiped Cari and Mare into loving them. It is the only way my two brilliant sisters would fall for such fiends.

Cari flashes me a toothsome grin, complete with

fangs. Marechal, only a couple of years older than me, gives me the maternal smile I've seen all my life. She hasn't been turned. Yet.

"Come inside." Marechal beckons.

The two women move into the dark recesses of the house. I hesitate, even though I know how the lore works. Humans don't need an invitation to come into the realms of monsters. It's getting out that's the trick.

"I wish you had called first," says Marechal. "We're headed out. Gaius has a political meeting."

"Political?" I say as we move into a formal living room. Doric columns frame the lit fireplace. Colorful murals line the walls around the curtained windows.

"Not with humans," says Cari, her voice reaching the excited pitch she uses when she is about to go on an adrenaline-inducing adventure. "A vampire delegation has come from Africa to meet with the guys at Club Toxic."

I clench my teeth at the use of the words *delegation* and *vampire* together. The word *politics* does not belong in the same sentence with such mindless monsters. But another thing catches my attention.

"You're not going to that club," I say. "Neither of you."

"You do know she's over twenty-one, Arneis," says Marechal, jerking her thumb at Cari. "And it's just a costume party. Venetian themed. It sounds like fun."

Marechal and *fun* don't usually come up in the same sentence, either. My older sister had to be dragged out from her lab up until a week ago. But our family name has been dragged enough, thanks to Frangelico and the Serranos.

"You don't know what happens at Club Toxic," I say.

"Do you?" says Cari. Her large brown eyes are no longer that of a child's. The tilt of her eyebrow says that she could answer her own question. What has that devil Hadrian gotten my sister into?

Even though I know what she now is, I still have trouble reconciling the fact that my baby sister is a blood-sucking monster. My hand goes to the bite on my shoulder. My entire body flinches as I touch it.

Cari's gaze goes solemn as she witnesses what I'm doing. Guilt wracks her features. "They're not all like that, Arnie."

She's referring to the bloodsucker who attacked us both weeks ago. I've only recently begun to remember the white-haired demon, Domitia. Before that, I'd only seen her in my nightmares because the

Serranos had taken the memories of her biting me and of her kidnapping Cari from me. But those two vampires didn't realize just how strong a mind like mine is.

I remembered. Now I need to find a way to let everyone in the town—everyone in the world—know what walks amongst us. I need to find a way to expose them—the Serranos, Frangelico-—or what they are.

But how?

"Plans have changed, ladies." Gaius Serrano steps into the formal room. The man is dressed in a silk robe that likely cost more than the city budget I balanced. "Queen Malika moved our meeting to tomorrow. So we can go back to bed. Ah, Arneis. Would you like to come in for dinner?"

Serrano's gaze spreads wide. The flash of his white teeth sends me back in time to the blinding pain when that crazed bitch sank her teeth into my neck and ripped my skin. My hand goes back to cover my neck, and I take a step back.

"You're not getting a bite out of me."

"Arneis," Marechal says. "Manners."

"It's fine, *minou*," says Gaius. "Do not fear, my brother. I only eat your sister now."

"Gaius," says Marechal. "Manners."

"I'm not your brother."

Gaius doesn't argue with me. My sisters look disappointed that I didn't take the ancient Roman's olive branch. I've never gotten into bed with the corrupt, and I don't plan to now.

"I have some place I need to be," I say. "I'll call before I come over next time."

"Are you sure you can't stay, Arnie?" says Cari.

She looks so much like herself, but I can feel a new strength in her. It's unnatural.

"I'll call you later," I say. "There's something I have to do."

I hop in my car and drive out of the property. I know exactly what I have to do. There will be a gathering of vampires inside Club Toxic tonight. I'm going to get in and gather proof to expose them. But my evidence will be the light of truth, and not a photo out of context.

If I can push the vampires out of the closet, then I can clear my name. My constituents will know I'm not the deviant with unnatural lusts that gossip rag made me out to be. They'll be able to see for themselves that there truly are things that go bump in the night. I'll be raised back to my former glory in the eyes of the twenty-percent I need to get reelected. Hell, I might even be able to aim for higher office.

2

"It's much grayer than I expected," I say as I peer down, out of the window of the luxury hotel in Tucson, Arizona. "And flat."

Slate towers scrape the azure horizon, reminding me of the step pyramids of Egypt. Instead of the vibrant natural hues like oranges and reds and browns, these buildings are varying shadows in the night. The only hint of color is the mountain that sits off in the distance. Its carob peak is a backdrop to remind these humans that they are insignificant, temporary guests on this planet.

"What did you expect, Sanai? They still can't

figure out how my aunts and uncles built the pyramids."

I chuckle as I turn to Fayola. Her tiny braids are coiled tightly around her head. Not a single strand has gone astray, even as she wakes to this new night, very unlike my own hair that is wild and free. My thick tufts of hair radiate from my head like the rays of the sun; rays I haven't seen in almost two hundred years.

"I only hope the queen finishes her business quickly so we can get back to civilized society," Fay says as she glides away from the window.

The gold bangles which cover the lengths of her arms make a tinkling sound, like a fanfare of bells announcing royalty is present. The gold accents warm her toasty brown skin. Her eyes are kohled in the way of her ancient ancestors. Her simple white sheath molds to her svelte form. Her head is high atop her long, ibis-like neck. The people here would call her a swan. She has the beauty and grace of the bird.

"Perhaps the Queen Mother will let us go on an excursion to Hollywood," I say.

Fay's regal features turn sour. "Why would we want to go there?"

I don't bother to respond. Fay doesn't like to

travel anywhere outside of Orun, the hidden queendom in the heart of the Saharan desert. The seat of power of the vampire queen, Malika.

Fay balked when I had a movie projector bought in at the turn of the twentieth century. She wouldn't go near the television box I set up fifty years ago. And she petitioned the queen about not allowing the internet inside the palace. So, I had to hoof it out into the desert with a satellite to catch up on reality TV each week.

"You look at this trip as an adventure, Sanai. When what it truly is, is business. We are here to do our duty to our Queen and the queendom," Fay says.

I'm still gazing out the window, so Fay doesn't see my eye roll. She's old school, as in five hundred years old. This place, these people, their innovations, are insignificant in her mind. It all was dust when she was reborn, and it will be but dust again when she takes her last breath. If it's not gold or the Egyptian engineering of her pharaonic ancestors, Fayola pays it little mind.

"The Queen Mother is here for diplomatic relations with King Lucius," Fay continues.

"Really?" I turn from the awakening nightlife out the window with a grin. "Because I hear that there is a party going on at his club for the next two nights."

"That is not our way; mixing with males, and humans."

By *males*, Fay means any males, be they vampire or, worse, human. There are very few males inside the queendom of Orun. Any who enter the palace are required to leave their most treasured appendage behind. Only eunuchs live and work in Queen Malika's sanctuary.

The queendom of Orun is comprised of the Queen Mother and her three princesses. Princess Fayola, a descendant of Princess Hatshepsut who became King of Egypt. Princess Eshe, a descendant of the Warrior Queen Njinga of the southern African nation of what is present-day Angola. And me, a descendant of Queen Amina in what is known in the present day as Nigeria.

The people of our nation came from the East when the Arabs raided villages as far back as the seventh century, as well as from the West when Europeans landed on our shores centuries later. Queen Malika slew all the slave traders she could get her claws on. She freed as many of the captured as she could. Now, she provides a safe harbor in Orun to any woman and child. Men she looks on with utter suspicion, unless they are willing to pay her the ultimate tribute.

"Fornication and coitus are for animals and humans," Fay continues.

I've seen that for myself. Animals spend all day rutting in the fields. Humans make a lot of films and videos that feature screwing. They make as many home improvement videos featuring nails and hammers as they make of people getting nailed and hammered.

"We are called for a higher purpose in this life."

I know she's right. But sometimes, I simply want to get in touch with my lower, base needs. Like, perhaps see a male vampire for the first time. See a real, live penis. Not a human one, of course. I'd never lower myself to sleep with one of those hairless apes.

But a virile, male vampire? With a throbbing cock? And a live vein that I could tap? Just the thought makes both my fangs and my loins ache.

"I'm off for my dinner," says Fay. "Are you joining me?"

"I'm not hungry," I say as I lick my fangs.

Fay heads out to slake her thirst. My stomach waits until she's gone before it growls with need. I'm not hungry for any of the limp dick eunuchs we brought along on this transcontinental journey. They avert their gazes when I feed from them, even when I wear low tops and my breasts swell over the fabric. They have no zest for life, and so they taste bland. For the first time in my life, I want to know what a real man tastes like.

If I can just find a way to get to Lucius Frangelico's party, I could find a thriving vampire male to slake my lust and maybe even my thirst with. But first, I'd need to find a way to slip past goody-two-shoes Fay's notice. And I'd also have to get past the queen, who notices everything.

As if she heard my thoughts, the doors to my suite open. I turn to see the queen entering with two of her attendants, young males who are large, with muscles. Their eyes are glazed over as most males who have had their manhood taken are.

"Sanai, *hartlam*, you should be resting."

Unlike Fayola, Queen Malika doesn't glide. She stalks into any space she occupies, like a lioness looking down on the bounty of animals she's considering taking a bite out of. She calls her three daughters *hartlams*, an amalgamation of heart and lamb. We were each given to her by our families, lambs to the slaughter, to whom she fed her heart's blood to turn us into vampire princesses to rule at her feet.

I bow my head as I address her. "I'm eager to begin the work we've come here for."

As the youngest of my sisters, I am only here to

observe. Eshe has the reign of the queendom while we're away. It is Fayola who is being groomed for these diplomatic talks, though Fay has no taste for small talk, traveling, or anyone other than her queen and sisters.

As I'm two hundred, the Queen Mother doesn't think I have enough experience of the world to handle our affairs on my own. I am hoping to prove her wrong on this trip. Which is going to be difficult if I get caught sneaking out tonight. But, priorities. As long as I can tag along to her meeting tonight with the vampire king, I'm certain I can sneak away for a second during the talks, to get the sneak peek of real life outside the dry desert that I crave.

"That will have to wait until tomorrow," says the queen. "The journey has made me tired."

I raise my lowered head and gape at the queen. She isn't looking at me. She's gazing at one of her guards with a hungry glint in her dark eyes.

"I'd prefer to have a nice dinner and then rest," she says. "I've sent a message to the Serranos, but I was unable to get one to King Lucius. The telephonic at his den only rings and rings. I came looking for Fayola to deliver the message personally."

"I can do it."

I swallow down the eagerness in my voice, but it is too late. I'm sure she heard it. She doesn't miss anything. But to my surprise, Queen Malika nods.

"You are a growing girl. I should give you more responsibilities."

She hands me a card. On it are gold embossed letters with red trim. It reads *Club Toxic*, along with an address.

"This is the location of Lucius's den. I believe he has a private room reserved for our use. Cancel it, and make sure we are not charged."

"As you wish, my queen."

I bow low, as low as I can go, so that she can't see the hungry gleam in my eye. When I rise, I go straight to my suitcase to find something to wear. I'm about to get up-up in da club.

3

Arneis

The masked goblins and superheroes have all gone inside for the night to gorge on their bounties in the safety of their homes. But the streets of downtown Tucson still teem with creatures of the night. Outside, the adult versions of superheroes with bare chests and barely covered nipples are all up to no good. But inside Club Toxic, the costumes are black and white and from a time long past.

I take a moment to admire the Venetian theme of the party. It's like something the upper crust of Tucson would put on. The men are in dark suits, some with a hint of white lace and frills. The women are in ballgowns and corsets, though most dresses are either form-fitting or barely there.

It was easy to throw together an outfit for this party. I simply had to go into my everyday closet. Black suits and ties are my mainstays. What I am missing is the mask.

"Councilman Durand."

I grimace at the sound of my name, then wince at the sight of the man who said it. Jared Johnson stands at what I now know is the hidden entrance to the underbelly of Club Toxic.

"Thought you learned your lesson the first time," says the beefy bouncer with tattoos like a sleeve down one arm.

"Times must be hard in the warehouse district if you're bouncing here instead of in the ring of your own club."

I had a hand in shutting down the fighting ring Jared and his buddies had set up. But they'd figured out how to make the operation legal, something I'm sure Frangelico was involved in. That must be why the man is here tonight protecting the Vampire King's assets. Jared isn't a vampire. I've seen him in the light of day. But he might be something else. Not only have I witnessed women with fangs and men who can wipe memories, I've seen people shift into jaguars.

Jared lets out a low growl as he eyes me. But his features shift from a menacing frown into an amused smirk. "I guess you're the Serranos' pet, with those brothers tapping both your sisters'... veins."

I clench my fist. I didn't come here to get into a fight. I have an agenda, as any good follower of Robert's Rules of Order should.

Before coming in, I reviewed the minutes of my last meeting. It had been difficult before a week ago, because I'd had my memory wiped. But now I remember everything. I can't get the image of Domitia sinking her fangs into my neck out of my mind. When I try, my vision clouds with my blood running down her chin, and then her carting my sister away.

I give my head a shake and focus on the mountain in front of me. The next item on my agenda is the roll call, the taking of attendance. "Where's Frangelico?"

"He's not available at the moment."

But he is here somewhere. I need to find him to tick off the next item on my agenda: the unfinished business between us.

"You can wait in the Serranos' private room, seeing as you're part of their family now."

That grates. I would never claim those blood-suckers as family. As soon as I have proof of this world, I'll get them away from my sisters. But I have to get the evidence first.

I pat the breast pocket of my shirt. The pin containing the spy camera is in place. It's online, feeding both sounds and images to a server back in my office.

Thanks to that news article, my word has been muddied. But the public can't argue with live video. I just need to get down to the floor below.

The last time I was here, I tried to do things by the book. Now, I am stooping to another level. It is all that's left to me to protect my family—hell, to protect the world. Mankind needs to know that these creatures—vampires, animal shifters, and who knows what else—walk amongst us, feeding off of us, stealing our livelihoods. I will out the scourge, and be labeled a hero. But first, I need to get inside.

Jared steps aside. He waves his thick arm, allowing me passage. I take a step towards the dark hall, but before I descend, something bright tugs at my attention.

I turn to look over my shoulder. Bodies are

gyrating on the dance floor. The faces of the humans above ground are contorted in grins of pleasure. They think they've found heaven on the dance floor. They don't realize hell is beneath their feet.

My gaze slides past the crowd at the center of the room, to the door. Coming into the entryway is an angel. She is light personified in the dark club. Her brown skin shines like this morning's sun rays did as they warmed the Catalina Mountains.

With each step she takes, she casts the club in shadows. The room pales into muted black and white, while she is a rainbow of color. She wears a ballgown just like the others on this night of Venetian revelry. There is a corseted bodice with ropes crossing over her chest. My fingers itch to play with the knots there, but my gaze dips to her flaring skirt where I'm sure a treasure is hidden. Her gown is an intricate pattern of oranges and reds and blues. It reminds me of the parades on Juneteenth, the African American celebration of emancipation.

She stops in the entryway. Her bright gaze looks from the floor to the ceiling as she takes in the club. Her elegant head pans on her swan-like neck as she takes in the crowd of dancers. I can see her chest inflate as she breathes in the excitement, desire, and alcohol in the air. If possible, her eyes go brighter, her grin splits wider.

I want to make a motion for the world to stop spinning. Inside my pants, my penis rises to second the motion. My head forgoes any need for debate. My heart thumps as hard as a gavel to bang the motion into law.

"Durand? You in, or you out?"

I blink, but she is still in my vision even as I turn back to Jared. For weeks, whenever I closed my eyes, I could only see that white-haired vampire and her fangs. Not this time. The vision of light and color shines in my mind. I turn back to the exterior doors, but she is gone.

The door to the lower level of the club stands open for me. I need only to walk down there and gather my evidence. Perhaps, when I come back up, I can find that glowing soul and get her out of this den of night creatures and to safety.

I take a step into the unknown and immediately wonder: *what the hell did I get myself into?*

On the other side of the wall is a live porn show, and not the kind to be found on a free site. This is what would be seen behind a paywall on the dark web.

Set against the red velvet of the furnishings are

men and women chained to crosses. The crystal chandeliers from above shine a light on their naked bodies. Some are bent over benches, taking a thrashing with hands, or long-tailed whips.

The problem is, none of what is happening is illegal. Even worse, there isn't a single fang or claw in sight for my camera to capture as irrefutable proof of the supernatural being real.

"Mr. Serrano?"

A pretty woman smiles at me. She has feline features. It wouldn't surprise me if there are cat shifters in the world.

I open my mouth to correct her on my name but decide against it, even though it grates. The Serrano name has got me this far. Hopefully, it will lead to pay dirt by the end of the night.

"Your private room is ready, if you'll follow me."

4

Sanai

It takes the darkness to cast the concrete city into color. Bright lights shine down onto the paved streets. Car horns roar as vehicles stampede up and down the way. Instead of the drab business suits and denim jeans I expected to see, the humans are out in spirited fashions.

Their ensembles include barely-there approximations of professional uniforms. Nurses with skirts the length of a Band-Aid. Maids with their nipples dusting over their tops. Firemen without their shirts, and police officers with their badges as the largest covering on their buff bodies.

The American celebration of Halloween has always baffled me. All over the continent of Africa, the different peoples celebrate their dead in a very different way. Of course, they dress in colorful garb and show off their tail feathers as all in the animal kingdom are wont to do. But the festivals' main purpose is to celebrate the dead and assure them that they haven't been forgotten. Not to offer candy to strangers dressed as skimpily as possible, and then try to get laid.

Hmmm. I think I like this way better.

"Happy Halloween, my beautiful African Queen," a man dressed in a cowboy costume yells at me as he raises his right fist.

I suppose it would be easy to take me for a queen based on what I'm wearing tonight. The bazin I'm wearing was handmade by the women of my mother's tribe. The strapless bodice hugs my breasts tight. The intricate knotting of the corset forces them to sit up high, but not high enough that my nipples dust over the top. The skirt flares from my hips in a cascade of oranges, reds, greens, and blues on a black background.

The patterns on the gown would bring to mind the kente cloth of West Africa. But the arrangement of the colors marks me as a princess, and not a queen. Still, I do not correct the good ole boy. Because one day, he'll be right.

Finally, I reach my destination. Club Toxic sits in the heart of the city. There is a line of humans trailing around the corner. The males wear dark suits with masks. The women wear tight gowns from a bygone era, or strategically placed leather with collars around their necks.

Oh yes, I definitely like this way of celebrating the dead better.

A man beckons me to the front of the line. I had been headed there anyway. I'm the daughter of Queen Malika of the Orun; all lines lead to me as my right.

"Good evening, Princess Sanai. I was told your party wasn't coming."

"I was sent to ensure you got that message. But since I'm here..."

His smile is crooked as he regards me. My nostrils twitch as I inhale. I've never smelled a male vampire before, but my instinct tells me he is something different. A dangerous beast; maybe a wolf?

Whatever he is, I see that he is taken. The gold band on his finger marks him as someone else's. So he likely won't be amenable to my plans for the night.

He reaches over and lifts the velvet rope. "Enjoy your evening, your highness."

I plan to do just that. I walk into the club and am hit with sensation overload. Outside the doors, the music had been a pleasant thump in my ears. Now, inside, the beat quickens my pulse. The smell of arousal and desire makes my mouth water.

We have regular dances at court where the people of our queendom gather to celebrate their savior and protector. During those performances, no man has ever gyrated against a woman in such a sexual manner. Certainly none has never put his hand there and kept his most treasured appendage.

A man walks up to me. He licks his lips as he regards me. His teeth are flat, not a fang in sight. So he doesn't want to bite me. He's moving his hips to the beat of the song.

Does he want me to dance? I don't know the steps. Looking out on the dance floor, I see there doesn't appear to be any coordination in the movements.

He must assume I'm shy or confused, so he puts his hand on my hip. I stiffen. The queen has always said that men are filthy creatures. I don't enjoy the sweaty smell of this one. But I'm here to have an experience.

His hand slides down my hip. When it snakes around the back, my patience for diplomacy comes to a screeching halt. I hiss, flashing my fangs. A crack sounds over the music, and I hear the cry of a little girl in pain. It's my dance partner. His arm is broken.

"Princess Sanai?"

I turn to find the large male who let me into the club looming over me. His hands are up, palms facing out towards me. It's a show of non-aggression.

"I'm sorry," I say, remembering the manners my human mother taught me before I became a vampire princess. "Was he yours?"

"Uh, no," the man says. He lowers his hands and his shirt shifts, revealing the tattoo of a wolf paw on his shoulder.

So, he is a wolf shifter. He makes a motion for me to hand over the handsy human. As I hand him over, I see there is a rip in my dress.

"I'll make sure Frangelico gets the bill for the damage. In the meantime, I believe your party is already here in the private room the queen requested."

Oh, the private room? That's what I'm supposed to ensure we aren't charged for. But the Serranos are already here? So, it appears we will be charged anyway. Might as well take the meeting. Perhaps I could ease the way for the queen's negotiations tomorrow night?

All around me, the party commences as though nothing happened. Humans rarely process things that don't please them. I'm taken to a hidden entrance at the side of the club. The curtains fall back and I am enveloped in red as far as the eye can see. But that's not what turns my fangs to sharp points.

I know of the sexual act. I've read about it in books, seen glimpses of it on the film recordings I've had smuggled into our desert oasis, and seen grainy and blurred snippets on the poor-quality internet I've dialed into. But I've never witnessed it live.

There's a lot of nudity. Women are naked, with tight nipples and reddened asses. There's also a nude male, his private parts under lock and key. I cock my head, trying to get a glimpse of his package to no avail.

"Mr. Serrano is just in here," says the woman who led me down into this well of sin. She has a button nose and perky ears that remind me of a kitten. I wonder if she's a cat shifter?

She said Mr. Serrano is here. One of the three infamous brothers is behind the door in front of me.

The escapades of those brothers during the time of the Spanish Inquisition is legendary. They were known to torture victims sexually, a method known to sweeten the blood of humans. A male such as that could easily seduce an innocent such as me. I should back away from this door and return to the sanctuary of my queen.

I reach past the tiny hostess and turn the knob myself. Beyond the doorway, I see the most delicious male I've ever encountered. His dark hair is tousled in a devil may care fashion. The fabric of his legs is molded to him, showing off his fit form. He wears a vest and jacket, but I can tell there is muscle beneath those layers.

Serrano takes me in, as well. His dark eyes start at the hem of my dress and travel upward. I have the urge to lift my skirts to give him a better look. My nipples harden when his gaze reaches my bodice. They push at the roped fabric, aiming to climb their way out of my top. A throb occurs between my legs when he reaches my eyes. I've been aroused reading books and fantasizing, but the feeling has never been this strong.

I want this man. I want him on me. I want him over me. My fangs ache to have his taste inside me.

Vampire lovers feed from one another. But I've

never had access to a male vampire. What will his blood taste like?

"You?" he says. "You work for Frangelico?"

"No. I work for no man."

His brow screws up in confusion.

"I'm here on my own."

His features still don't relax. I feel like I'm saying the wrong things. As I struggle with the right things, I've forgotten that we aren't alone in the room.

"You have the room until midnight. Enjoy."

The door shuts behind me. Then I hear the click of a lock. Midnight is hours away. That's more than enough time to allow this sexy vampire to seduce me.

5

Arneis

I hear the click of the lock as the door shuts. My mind is whizzing and whirring as I try to find order in this situation I find myself in. The angel from up above has been cast down into this pit of hell. Set against the white walls of the private room, she shines even brighter than when she was in the dim club.

Her brown skin is like that strong cup of coffee that unfailingly gets me through a long policy report filled with monotonous data and charts. My eyes drink her in and I am buzzed off the shot of dark roast.

She moves a step towards me and I get a hint of her sweet aroma. The tendrils of her scent curl into my nostrils, making me lift my feet off the ground and bringing me face to face with her. Eye to eye. Mouth to... what is she saying?

"Which one are you?"

There is a lilt to her voice. She elongates her vowels. Her teeth catch on the consonants like they would take a bite out of them. When she says my name, it will be all softness.

"Mr. Serrano?"

And just like that, my tongue tastes bitterness. But the acrid aftertaste clears my head and reminds me why I'm here: to get evidence of vampirism. That won't happen with this human woman.

Does she know where she is? Vampires can wipe memories. I know that first hand.

A smile curls at the edge of her lips. I watch the stretch of her flesh and feel the urge to touch it, to taste it, to bite it. Some of the whirring in my head stops as I take her in anew. The woman is the very definition of regal. There's an upwards tilt to her chin which I'm willing to bet she never lowers. Her lashes are winged spikes at the tips as though even her eyes hold a crown.

Her gown would cast that of any Disney princess

into the shade. Though when I look closer, I see there is a rip in the fabric of her dress. I take another step toward her, taking the ruined fabric in my hands.

"Did they hurt you?" I ask.

She looks down at the material in my hand. I realize how inappropriate my action is and release my hold, though my fingers clench into fists at the emptiness.

"A male tried to get fresh and I..." She purses her lips, as though holding in the words that were about to escape. Then she brushes the fabric back into place. "Management handled it."

Is she one of the sex slaves here? A beauty such as her—she would be a prize. Just looking at her, I feel I am going out of my mind with want.

"Are you a slave?" I ask.

This room was reserved for Gaius and Hadrian. Was this woman forced in here for those two vampires to feed from? Or, worse, have sex with? And what is pissing me off more? The fact that those bloodsuckers are cheating on my sisters? Or that they would lay a finger on this vision before me?

Her eyes flash. "No, colonizer. I'm not a slave. And I'll stake any man who tries to put me in the belly of a boat headed for the Atlantic."

"I'm sorry." I wince. "I didn't mean... What I'm trying to say—"

"Though I might be talked into chains."

My gaze snaps back to her. She's no longer standing before me. She has walked to the corner of the room where rope, whips, and chains hang on the wall.

I didn't have much time to take in the room before she arrived. Now, I give the place a thorough investigation. At the center of the room is a cushioned table of the kind that might be found in a massage parlor. A tray holding what could only be sex toys sits in another corner of the room. Colorful dildos and vibrators are lined up like soldiers awaiting orders.

She runs her hands over the chains hanging from the wall. She scrapes her nails against the metal chains, and over coarse rope. My cock, which had already been stirring in my pants, rises to attention. It punches against the front of my pants when she places her hand on her chest, on the rope mesh that crosses her skin there. I have an urge to rip the bottom of her dress down and use the top to bind her.

I give my head a shake. I have no idea where that

thought came from. Does it make me racist to want to tie a Black woman up?

What I do know is that my thoughts make me no better than the people on the other side of that door. No one out on the floor looked as though they were doing anything against their will. But they may have had their will stolen from them.

I've learned that vampires can hold others in their thrall when you look them directly in their eyes. I look directly into her eyes. When I do, I feel lost, like I'm falling. What if she is under another's thrall? What if she is only here at a vamp's command?

"Why are you here?" I ask.

"I wanted to meet you." Her grin turns sheepish. The woman is fondling sex toys but only now does she seem to blush. "You're not what I expected."

Of course I'm not. I'm not one of the undead Serrano monsters. "What did you expect?"

"That you would pounce on me the moment the door was closed."

Pounce? Does she mean sexually, or hungrily? I have to assume she knows what the Serranos are. But my mind is too focused on the suggestion in her words.

"Is that what you want?" I ask.

She lets go of the chains. I watch her hands glide down her body and come to settle at her middle. She folds them together, her head bowed. I have a vision of her like that, on her knees. Her mouth level with my cock as I lift her chin with my index finger.

The thought rocks me back on my heels. Then I am rocked forward with how much I want that dream to become a reality. It's been a long time since I've been in a relationship. I've never been as randy for a woman as I am just looking at her.

She lifts that proud chin up. "What I want is—"

There is a hiss from the other side of the room. She turns and backs into me. I wrap an arm around her, ready to protect her from any danger. But the danger isn't in front of her, it's behind her. My cock punches the front of my pants as her skirts brush against me.

A curtain opens to reveal a scene on the other side of the glass. Before us is the floor of the underground sex club. I'm sure the mirror is one way because no one is looking in at us. All eyes are on the scene on the floor.

A naked woman kneels while a fully-clothed man paces around her. The woman bares her neck. The male flashes his fangs. He nicks her finger, and laps up the blood trickling there.

With that little show, my camera has caught what I need. I have evidence of the existence of vampires.

I can leave now. But my feet are rooted to the spot in this private room. Not because I'm interested in the show on the other side of the glass. But because I'm attuned to the woman standing in front of me.

She steps back into me. I hiss as her ass full on grazes my cock. She stiffens and turns to glance over her shoulders.

"You have an erection," she says, surprise in her voice. "Is that because of me? Or because of the show?"

I'm having trouble finding my voice. She's still pressed against me. Her voice is in my ears. And now her scent is in my nose. It's too much for any man to be able to function.

"I've never aroused a man before," she says turning slowly until she faces me. "The queen doesn't allow virile men in the palace. Can I touch it?"

6

____

Sanai

The bulge in his pants fascinates me. I can see it snake and uncoil like a viper against the dark fabric. He hisses in a gasp as I take a step. His body tenses, as though preparing to strike. Can he sense that I will bare my flesh for his bite?

I take another step, enthralled by the danger pulsating between his thighs. It pulses, like a drum, against the front of his pants. My body begins to sway in time to its beat. I reach my hand to him, but he grasps my wrist. I glance up into his face.

There's a mix of desire and shock there. His gaze is narrowed on me, but his dark eyes gleam in the dimly lit room. His lips are pulled back from his teeth, but his teeth are clenched. His skin is flushed, a redness touches his strong cheekbones. He must have eaten recently.

That thought bothers me. I hear that male vampires bite their lovers during the sexual act. I have only ever been bitten by the Queen Mother during my turning. It was an experience that I would be happy to forget.

"I don't understand why you're so surprised," I say. "Your reputation precedes you. Serranos are known for their sexual exploits."

"I'm not—"

His voice is choked as he tries to speak. It sounds dry, as though he is thirsty. I step closer, tilting my head to the side and baring the column of my throat. But when he looks at my offering, his expression is pained.

I snatch my hand out of his grasp and take a step back. A flush creeps across my cheeks. "You're not interested in me?"

The thought hadn't even entered my brain before this very moment. In the palace, the jewel-less males all avert their gazes from my sisters and me. In the village beyond the castle, I know the males look at my form. But only under the cover of their lashes, and from a distance, never up close and directly.

There were plenty of people who looked like me at the time he was born in Rome, as well as during his escapades during the Spanish Inquisition. But perhaps my looks are not to his tastes?

I look nothing like the wispy, pale-skinned women on the streets. Or the one who is on her knees on the other side of the glass between the two males, as one kisses her mouth and the other kisses her breasts. I don't have the experience of being kissed, let alone the knowledge of what it's like to be with one man.

I should probably get out of this room and have my first experience with a human instead of a half-millennium-old vampire. I must look like a child at play to him.

"You're the most beautiful thing I've ever seen in my life," he says.

"What did you say?"

His voice still sounds hoarse, so I'm not entirely sure I heard him correctly. That's not true. My hearing is superior. I know what he said; I just want him to say it again.

He opens his mouth to speak. My body sways towards him, eager to gulp down a second helping of his words. Of their own accord, my fingers uncoil and, quick as a snake, they strike out and cup his manhood.

Instead of saying the words I long to hear, he hisses again. His breath is a spicy mist that hits my nostrils. His eyes slide closed, and his lips spread into a grimace of ecstasy.

"I have never felt such power," I say as I handle him. He is thick in my palm. I cannot gather the fullness of his length in my hand. He spills over the edges of my thumb and pinky finger. "I wonder if this is why the queen cuts them off?"

My back is flung against a wall. With one hand, he moves my hand from the front of his pants and presses it over my head. The fingers of his other hand weave into the laces of my corset, and he cups my breasts. I hiss out a breath of pure pleasure. No one has ever touched me there.

"I must be out of my mind," he says. His lips hover just over mine. "This is not what I came here for."

"This is exactly what I came here for," I say. "To meet you."

His gaze travels over my face. Those dark eyes linger on my lips, and I can feel their heat. "I'm not who you think I am," he says.

"You're not one of the Serrano brothers?"

He winces as he meets my gaze. "Technically, yes. I am."

I don't think I'd care if he wasn't. I want him. I'd thought any man would do, but I wouldn't trade places with the woman on the other side of the glass. She has two men's hands on her. And they're...

Well, that's interesting.

On the other side of the glass, one of the men continues to kiss the woman on her mouth. The other one is spreading her thighs before he goes to his knees, and then he puts his mouth on her... there.

I didn't know such a thing was done. Her body is trembling, from her head down to her toes, which are bouncing off the floor as both men lap at her orifices.

"I want to kiss you," says Serrano.

My chest heaves. I want him to kiss me too. But now I'm thinking of kissing in a whole new light.

I turn back to him just in time to meet his lips. He's pressing his hard body into me, but his lips are soft. I'd expected roughness. He is a man, after all. But he handles me with care.

His lips speak of urgency as they press into mine.

But each brush is a whisper. Each touch, a sigh. It makes me want him more.

When his tongue sneaks out of his mouth and licks at my upper lip, my body sings a new tune. When his teeth tug at my lower lip, I hear the drums again. The pulsing beat of him fills my ears. I want to dance with him. To shimmy my chest and shake my hips. Preferably while on top of him.

I would let this man bite me if he wanted. I want him to let me bite him. I want to know what he tastes like. But I know that blood exchange between two vampires is a delicate dance, so I take his kiss and pray for patience as the rhythm intensifies.

Arneis

It's been a while since I've kissed a woman. A long while. So long, in fact, that I can't remember the name of the last woman I kissed. Or her face.

My vision is fogged over with ebony clouds as I run my hands through her hair. I dig my fingers into the soft tufts of her coiled locks, and feel like I'm floating. Pulling her close, I anchor her body to mine. If I am going to sail away, it's going to be while I'm moored to this exquisite creature in my arms.

I'd forgotten how soft a woman's lips are. Or is that just her softness?

I'd forgotten the velvety warmth of a woman's tongue. Or is that just her heat?

I want to investigate every crevice of her. I want to take my time and explore her valleys and curves. But she is anxious in my hold, impatient.

Her body moves against mine, more like an oncoming storm than a sedate, fluffy cloud on a sunny day. Her moans are a thunderous pleading. Her eyes flash open, and the desire inside strikes like lightning.

I pull away to catch my breath. However, both my body and her lips protest. A low, keening cry comes from the other side of the glass. We are both momentarily distracted as we turn to see a new scene.

A woman is being tied up. The man who binds her is dressed in black. The rope in his hands is golden. The woman doesn't fight the confinement. Her eyes are glazing over as though the golden strands are an extension of her lover's caress. The brilliant strands are zigzagging streaks against the black of her dress; like contained lightening.

"Please," says the beam of light before me.

The sound of her begging flips a switch in me. I want to hold her captive so that I can taste the fire inside her. I want to bind her to me while I thrust into the eye of her storm. I want to catch lightning in a bottle, and I don't care if I get burned.

On the other side of the glass, the cries of pleasure have turned to gargled pants as the man face-fucks the woman he's bound. I worry the poor woman is choking, but she tilts her head back for more. It looks depraved. It looks dirty. It looks demeaning.

"Please," says the spark of radiance in my arms.

Suddenly, I want to tip her head back by her chin and shove my cock down that elegant throat of hers.

I don't know where these thoughts are coming from. All of my past girlfriends were conservative in the carnal department. Missionary twice a week was good enough for them. They barely touched my cock with their hands, much less had it anywhere north of their stomachs. I've never gone down on a woman.

Now my mouth hungers for it. My tongue aches for it. My lips part, ready to take it.

I back away from the temptation trapped in this room with me. But I don't go far. I reach for the rope on the wall. When I turn back, her breathing is shallow as she eyes the ends of the twine swinging in my hand.

"Sit down," I say.

She does as I command. Her slender fingers gather the fabric of her gown. She lifts the material as she places herself onto the cushioned table. I am treated to the sight of her lean ankles, and a hint of her sculpted calf. My fingertips tingle, and I haven't even touched her yet.

I come to kneel before her with rope in hand. I take her left calf and position it to the metal leg of the massage table. Then I unravel the corded rope.

The corded braid hits the floor. The light thumps match the pounding of my heart, as well as the pulsing of my dick as it anticipates what I am about to do. Luckily, I was an Eagle Scout. I know how to tie a knot.

I crisscross the ropes over her skin. The pattern isn't as pretty as that of the man who bound the woman outside, but the clove hitch knot will serve my purpose. It will join her leg to the bedpost, and will hold her captive while I explore the depraved thoughts racing through my head.

"What's your name?"

"Sanai."

"That's beautiful," I say as I take her right calf into my palm. Her skin is smooth in my hand, but I feel a zap of energy skate across my knuckles.

"It means brilliance."

I look up at Sanai, and grin. She smiles down at me. In the darkened room, I feel I am drowning in sunlight.

"Call me Arneis."

"What does that mean?"

"It's a type of grape found in the hills of Roero in Italy." I finish the loop and give the rope a tug, tightening its hold on her leg, ensuring she cannot escape. "It translates to *little rascal*."

I reach for the edges of Sanai's gown. Slowly, I slide the dress up. The gown had flared about her legs like a mermaid's tail. As I raise it, the black trim of the fabric bunches into the splashes of red as her kneecaps are revealed. The blue patterns of the design fold into the green stencils as the tops of her thighs are bared to me.

I have been between a woman's thighs. But I've only ever aimed my cock and thrust. I have never actually looked.

With her ornate gown gathered at her waist, I move my hands to Sanai's knees to spread her apart. Her lace black panties hide nothing from my eyes. The lush decadence of her scent knocks me back on my heels, and that's when I realize my folly.

How am I going to get her panties off without untying her? Because I have no intention of setting this woman free until I've had my fill of her. Possibly, not even after that.

I reach for the lace with unsteady fingers. Above me, Sanai's breathing increases. I've never had a woman want it this much before. Her desire only fuels me.

Fuck it. I take the thin scrap of lace between both of my thumbs and index fingers, and I pull. The scrap of material easily gives way, and leaves me with no further obstruction to my desires.

There is truly nothing between me and the lips I want to kiss. Sanai is completely shaved. Brown skin meets the darkest pink, and my mouth waters. All thought stops, and I can only feel. And the first thing I feel is those lips of hers on mine.

8

In my culture, back two hundred years ago when I was born, nudity was not dwelled upon. Both men and women walked around half, or sometimes fully, bared with no thought of others. Leering, rape or other sexual violence was unheard of as it was punishable by the gods—namely a vengeful matriarch who would rip a perpetrator's throat out with her teeth.

It was only after I was given in offering to Queen Malika that I came to believe that my body was special. That it was blasphemy for a man to look upon even my face, much less my bared chest.

Right now, I spread my thighs for Arneis.

My knees quiver with anticipation at what he'll do. I know what he'll do. He's going to lick me between my legs, a place that's never been touched before. Not even by me.

But he's not touching me yet. He only stares, gazing at the heated flesh between my thighs. I feel myself growing wet under his attention. I can tell he likes what he sees. His breaths are shorter, shallower, like a cheetah who has chased down his prey and is stalking closer, preparing to sink his teeth in.

My hips jerk at the thought of Arneis's fangs piercing my flesh.

"Hold still," he says. "I want to remember every detail of this moment."

He gives a tug on the rope, tightening my ankles to the posts. I'm strong enough to break the knots and the clever ties with a kick. I'm sure he knows this. I don't think the physical restraint is the point of this exercise. I think he wants me to hold still of my own free will. The bindings are likely there as a reminder that I am under his power. He is hundreds of years older than me, and could easily overpower me.

Just the thought thrills me. I have never been submissive to a man. It's not in my nature. But being bound by this man, following his commands, I feel as though I am evolving in real-time.

The cries of the woman on the other side of the glass pierce my ears. She, too, is bound and at the mercy of the male towering over her. Her head is bowed as he thrusts into her body from behind. Her eyes are glazed over in pure ecstasy. If that's what I'll receive for handing my will over to this man, I am ready to be bound from head to toe.

Arneis dips his head between my spread thighs. The light stubble on his cheek grazes the sensitive flesh there. My breath catches as he exhales and a warm breeze rustles my intimate skin. He hasn't even gotten to his final destination yet, but I am ready to submit. He's overpowered me with just the thought of what he's about to do.

In anticipation, my right leg bounces against the leg of the cot. In excitement, my heel rises and I go up on the ball of my foot. I feel the rope against my leg. It presses into my skin in a warning that I do not heed. And then I hear twine snap.

Arneis's head pulls back, all the way back to my knees. His dark gaze latches onto mine. I want to beg for forgiveness. I want to plead for another chance.

"I'll be good," I say, pressing my freed leg back against the cot's post. "I'll hold still."

A grin spreads across his handsome face. I feel like a pet who just got the praise of its master. This man is about to own me. I'd be down on my knees panting for a treat if I weren't so focused on keeping those same knees apart.

There's no more dawdling. Arneis pushes my knees apart, as far as they'll go while in the rope's grasp. I feel a puff of his hot breath. Then the nuzzle from the tip of his nose. And then the velvety wetness from the tip of his tongue.

My head falls back. I struggle to keep myself upright, but my arms want to collapse in surrender. He only gives a few tentative licks before his lips close around mine and he's sucking at me.

The pleasure is unlike anything I've ever known. Unlike anything I could've imagined. I'd always thought a male's penis went into the vagina. He's putting his tongue in mine. Does the queen know about this? If she did know, none of the servants would be able to speak from the loss of their tongues.

Arneis laps at me like I'm fruit. My heels are off the floor again. I cannot help it. But I keep my knees wide for him. The last thing I want is for him to stop.

I dig my nails into the cot, feeling the plastic

covering give way under my nails. I'm shaking now. A deep pressure is building inside of me. The weight of it started in my core, but I feel it radiating outward. Gravity is reversing inside of me as Arneis's hot tongue moves from my most secret entrance to the tip of my sex.

He encircles that small bud first with his tongue, then with his lips. When his teeth graze the bundle of nerves, my world turns upside down. The force that was holding my inner world together lets go, and I crash.

My thoughts scatter as I scream my pleasure. My arms give way, and I collapse back onto the cot. I want to press my legs closed, to try to contain the pulsing from within that has yet to recede. Surely, I can't take much more of this. I'm going to drown if the waves of bliss continue this assault.

But I can't close my legs. Something is obstructing me. Or rather, someone.

Arneis has not stopped licking me. He suckles me harder, causing the waves to surge once more and pull me deeper down into delirium. I'm nearly out of my mind, but I do not come out of the remaining binding on my leg. I do not want him to stop.

He doesn't stop. He inserts a finger into my core, where his tongue already eased the way. The pressure that was still crashing over me increases. I can't believe it's possible but it builds, rising even higher. The pressure that is building feels different this time. Its weight doesn't feel solid, it feels liquid.

Arneis works his fingers in and out of my core as he licks. He crooks his finger. Like a pirate using a treasure map, his fingers hit a spot. The pressure crashes against me again, but this time, I feel moisture trickle down my legs as my body convulses.

Oh no. Have I embarrassed myself? My bladder wasn't full when I came in. The liquid isn't golden. It's clear, and Arneis is lapping it up as it continues to pour from me.

My inner muscles clench around his fingers. My pussy grabs for his tongue. My incisors sharpen.

His eyes are closed as he moans and laps at me. He is pulling my essence from me. Perhaps my very soul.

I need him in my mouth. His cock. His neck. Anything of him. But he is not stopping his licking. I am shaking uncontrollably when he pulls another bout of the clenching pleasure from me.

That is it. I can take no more. I kick free of the

bindings. I go to reach for him when he sits back on his haunches and unbuckles his pants. My gaze fixes on the treat he unwraps for me.

The head of his cock is pulsing red with desire. I want to sink my teeth into it.

9
______

Arneis

I'm not a man given to wanting more than my fair share. I didn't grow up with a silver spoon in my mouth. I grew up with a silver cork in my hands. With a twist of my wrist, I can unscrew any vintage stored in any bottle.

But tonight, with the curves undulating in my hands, I am completely screwed.

I am drunk on Sanai's taste. Not tipsy. Beyond intoxicated. My brain is addled on the taste of her. I am falling down, fucked up, and thirsty for more.

I've never had a woman come on my tongue. I've never put my tongue on a woman, but I couldn't help myself. Even as I pull away from her, I want more. Her orgasm was so powerful that she shook loose my knot at her ankle.

The need to be inside her consumes me. The night of firsts continues for me. My first time tying up another human being. My first time eating a woman's pussy. My first time fucking on the first date.

If this were any other night, I would've gotten her phone number. I would've called, in the evening, after work. We would've chatted about our work, our goals in life, what our current retirement portfolio was comprised of. The normal getting to know someone banter.

This isn't a normal night. She is not an average woman. I am not my orderly, rule-abiding self. Things are out of order, and I wouldn't have them any other way.

I pull back from Sanai, trying to figure out how to unbuckle my pants. She sits up, her gown falling over her spread legs and hiding those lush lower lips from my view.

I want to growl at her to stay put. But she steps down from the padded table. She is on her knees, her face level with my straining cock. The sight of Sanai crawling towards me is burned forever into my soul. It will be the only thing I want to see for the rest of my days.

Her hand goes to my cock. I can't even remember taking it out of my fastened pants. Somehow, it found its own way to her.

"Please," she says. "May I?"

She tilts that proud chin of hers back. The golden sparkle in her dark eyes flashes at me. My dick lifts up, my hips thrust towards her.

I have never had a woman suck my cock before. Not any of the prim misses I have dated ever did it. It was something you would ask a prostitute or a mistress to do. Since I'd never had or planned to have either, I'd never considered the act.

Sanai carries herself with a regal air. She is destined to be a trophy on some lucky man's arm. A savage part of me is willing to kill for the honor of being that worthy male.

Right now, she's looking at my dick like it's the trophy. I have just buried my thighs between her legs. I'm a staunch supporter of equal opportunity for women. So...

Her first lick makes my toes curl in my shoes. When she wraps those perfect lips around the head, I have to reach behind her to use the massage table for balance. I am a man who is always in control. But when I feel the scrape of her incisors against my sensitive flesh, I nearly spend in her mouth.

The thought of a bite, in a place like this, should send me reeling back into the dark recesses of my mind. Back to the horror-laced vision of a white-haired demon taking a pound of flesh and blood from me. But Sanai's accidental graze has my balls tightening.

Maybe I've developed a fetish as part of my PTSD from the incident? I am having sex in the den of a vampire nightclub, with a woman I only met less than an hour ago. A woman who makes me feel like I'll die if I don't come inside her.

Sanai protests as I pull her off my cock. She releases my dick with a pop. The spark in her gaze is now fire.

"I need to be inside you," I say.

"You were just inside me." Her tone is saucy, her lips in a petulant frown.

"Get back on the table." My voice is low, hard. I'm running low on patience, and I need her to obey me. "Now."

Her breath catches. The fire in her eyes ignites. She likes being bossed around. Good, because I need her to hold still while I fuck her senseless.

Sanai lifts her gown and prowls backward onto

the table. My gaze latches onto the flushed skin between her legs. It still glistens from my earlier attention.

My hands find the rip in her dress. I take the ruined fabric and tear out a strip. Sanai gasps at my handiwork, but she does not protest. I use the material to bind her hands together. This time, I tie a butterfly knot. The loops of the knot, along with the colors of the fabric, adorn her skin, and make my dick even harder.

Once she's bound, I kneel between her thighs. Part of me wants to rip the entire gown to shreds and refashion the design by tying her down to the table. But my cock is impatient.

I don't have a condom, and I realize I don't care. I know I'm clean because I haven't been in a relationship for months. If she has something, I'll catch it too, because there is no way I'm not getting inside this woman. If a child results...

The thought knocks some sense into me. Not the sense to pull the head of my cock away from her entrance. It knocks me flush up against her swollen lips. Because the thought of this woman with her belly swollen with my babe is the most erotic thing ever.

I push into her. At first, the way is easy. She is still slick from my tongue. She is also tight.

Sanai winces as I breach her flesh. I hope to God she's not hurt, because I don't want to stop. I can't stop.

Her inner walls don't try to push me out. Her muscles grab hold of me, trying to suck me deeper inside. I oblige, and push in further.

Sanai gasps. Her eyes are wide with what looks like surprise. Her lips part, and a low moan escapes her mouth.

My brain is so fogged over with desire and ecstasy that I can't remember the difference between the sound of pain and the sound of pleasure. Pulling out of her exquisite channel is unfathomable. But so is the thought of causing this woman any pain.

When her legs wrap around my ass, I know she likes it. When she lifts her hips to meet my thrusts, I know she wants more.

"Deeper," she begs.

I oblige. There is no more resistance as I slide all the way into her warm depths. My balls rock up against her ass. I pull her hips down, trying to gain another inch deeper inside of her.

Sanai's back arches off the table, and a shudder ripples through the length of her body. I feel her toes curling on the back of my calf. Her knees press into my hips. Her flat stomach trembles as she exhales a sigh of contentment. Her bound arms stretch over her head, and her fingers unfurl and reach out.

"Harder," she pleads.

I've never taken a woman roughly before. But the suggestion sounds like the perfect order of business. I withdraw slowly, feeling the clutching of her inner walls along the way. Once only the tip remains inside her, I ram back to where I came from in one swift thrust. We both cry out at the impact.

I continue to drive into her. She lifts her hips to meet my movements, impaling her tight sheath on my shaft. Her words make no sense, like she's speaking in tongues. But somehow I am able to understand every one of her entreaties.

I take her fast, hard, deep. I do not stop. Not even when she is shaking with another orgasm.

Her hands pull against the binds, but she doesn't break that knot. The sight of this woman pinned beneath me as I thrust into her is all I want for the rest of my days.

I want to hold her still while I give her more pleasure than she can handle. I want her to behave while I have my way with her. I want to take my fill of her so that I can give her what she needs.

I can feel my climax coming. When her sex clenches around me with another orgasm, I let go. I throw my head back and roar as my seed shoots into her.

It is bliss. I feel complete, whole where I didn't know something had been missing. But something is still missing.

I feel Sanai's hands on my back. When did she break free of the bindings? How did she break free?

She smiles at me, a dazed look in her eyes. Then I catch it. Something sharp in her mouth glints in the dim light of the room.

Fangs.

She's still moving against me, her core still pulling at my semi-hard dick. She opens her mouth and strikes my neck.

My mind struggles to understand what's happening. The beautiful angel I want to be the mother of my children is feeding from me. It should be wrong. But it feels so right.

There is a pinch of pain when her teeth pierce the skin at my neck. Something tells me to jerk away from the pain. To break free. To run.

A louder voice in my head tells me not to. I listen to that voice. Sanai's lips wrap around the point where she's punctured my skin. She pulls at the jugular vein in my neck, and it's a total knock out.

The bliss pulls me under as her tongue laps at my skin. She moans around the wound she's given me as she takes her sustenance. My dick comes alive inside her channel. With her next sip of my blood, my body explodes in another orgasm.

All resistance goes out of me as I come hard, harder than a moment ago. With her inner muscles pulling at my dick and her mouth pulling at my vein, I am lost. But something keeps whispering in my mind.

It's something important that I should be wary of. Something that keeps trying to worm its way between me and this woman. This creature. This...

Vampire.

10

———

Sanai

is blood is like nothing I've ever tasted. I've had many men on my tongue. But none of them were virile and full of life. Apparently, something gets taken from a male when his manhood is snipped. The moment Arneis Serrano's blood hits my tongue, I know that I will never be satisfied with another man's again, regardless of whether that blood donor is intact or not.

As his potent blood slides down my throat, I feel another orgasm rising inside me. This time, when I find my release, it's not just my body that shivers. My entire spirit explodes, like a supernova that recedes and leaves me with a new, shining soul.

I've lived for two hundred years, but now I feel alive. When my eyes open, I see new hues and tones in the colors of the world. My ears hear not only Arneis's heartbeat but the working of the valves that pump his delectable blood through his body. My mind feels like the grooves laid in my brain have been repaved with a new understanding of the world around me.

What I don't understand is why Arneis is pulling away from me.

Why is he looking at me with such horror on his handsome face?

Then it dawns on me. I should've known better than to take his blood without asking first. With a human, I have never asked. They have only ever been sustenance to me. But we vampires can't make our own blood, which is why we feed off of mankind.

I'm not sure how it works between two vampires who can't make their own blood. Will we need to have a human to replenish our stores? The idea of his mouth on another makes me see red: the human's spilled blood as I slit their throat.

Arneis backs away from me—scrambles, is more like it. He pulls up his pants as he does so.

"I'm sorry," I say. "I should've asked first."

"You're a vampire."

His words are not what I expected him to say. I was expecting a scolding. Perhaps I've been looking forward to a punishment. Maybe that's why I bit him without permission.

"Of course I am," I say. "Are you going to bite my ass as a punishment?"

I expect Arneis to flash his fangs at me. Instead, he grinds his molars. The look of disgust that he gives me chills the blood on my tongue. My saucy grin turns downward as I watch his lips curl.

I've never tasted another vampire's blood. I've only tasted eunuchs' blood. It's not possible that Arneis is human.

Is it?

"You're not—"

"A monster like you," he sneers.

Any hint of desire has fled from his features. His hand grazes his neck where I bit him. It comes away with a tiny smear of blood on his thumb.

My mouth waters at the sight. He catches it, and takes another step away from me. I pull my dress over my legs and tuck my knees under me.

It's true; he's human.

I have failed so hard tonight. I didn't do as I was told and cancel this room. It got used, and used well. And now I see I've given my virginity away, and not to an ageless vampire of a renowned line. But to a human male, no less. I was prepared to take some risks with my actions this night. The queen will cast me out when she learns how royally I've screwed up.

"You enthralled me," Arneis accuses.

My head snaps up at that. "I did no such thing."

"It's the only explanation." He tightens his belt, looping the leather inside the buckling and closing the clasp.

On the other side of the glass, the man is pounding into the woman. The sounds of her wet sex are louder than her cries and his grunts. But all I can hear is the disdain and disgust in Arneis's voice.

"I would never sleep with someone like you," he says.

"Someone like me?"

"It's not my first time being attacked by one of your kind."

"Attacked?"

Arneis's hand goes to his neck. Not the side where a few drops of blood trickle from my bite. There is a wound healed over on the other side of his neck. Whoever put it there was careless, as though they intended to cause him pain.

"Don't try to mind wipe me," he says, turning back to face me.

I've never tried the tactic. The humans in our hidden oasis know who and what we are. They keep our secrets. Outsiders have never found us out in the heart of the desert.

"You think I'd make you forget what happened between us?" I ask.

His gaze finds mine then. The anger and disgust slips. I see the man who desired me only moments ago. The man who was so deep inside of me that I couldn't remember what being apart from him was like.

I know he sees it too. But only for a second. And then he shutters himself to me.

"I recorded everything," he's saying, tapping a button on his shirt. "The feed has gone straight to a hard drive that's set to go live if I don't stop it."

With my sharp vision, I see that there are gears inside the object. A lens stares back at me. A camera has recorded what just happened between us. Meaning my first and only lover has recorded a sex tape of me. Could I be any more naive?

"Now the world will know about your kind."

It looks like I could be a bit more naive than I originally thought. Arneis will expose not only me, but the secrets of the vampire world. I won't have failed just my queen, I'll have failed my entire race of people. There's a part of me that worries he will be hunted down and killed if he shares any details of the supernatural world. But there's another part of me that hurts worse than that: shame.

"You'd put what we shared on display for the world to see?" I say.

Arneis's jaw tenses at that thought. Something proprietary goes over his features. His thumb fumbles as it rubs at the device on his shirt. The rest of his fingers scratch at his chest, where his heart beats.

I gaze into his eyes. I feel his will. He is strong. But I'm stronger.

I could do it. I could dive into his mind, tug at his will, and make him forget. I could make him do my bidding.

Arneis looks at me as if he knows what I'm thinking. His hand falls away from the device, from his heart. He holds still under my gaze, as though he's daring me to do it. Or willing me to.

We stare at each other for long moments, both unguarded as memories of the past hour replay in our minds. My channel aches from the loss of him. My fangs throb for another taste of him. My heart beats against my chest, urging me to close the distance between us.

I can hear his heart beating a rapid rhythm as well. I scent the arousal coming off his body. I see his hands clench around the air by his sides. And then I watch as he walks away from me and out the door without a word.

11

____

Arneis

She's a monster. That's what I keep telling myself as I drive away from the club. But my mind goes back to the look in her eyes when I'd called her that to her face.

She could have lashed out at me. Literally or physically. But she didn't.

At first, she'd seemed embarrassed by her actions. Apologetic, even. There had been hurt there.

Hurt that I put there. Sanai looked lost and small when she came to realize I was disgusted by who she is.

No. Not who she is. What she is.

She is a monster. A demon that feeds off of mankind for sustenance as well as amusement.

She kissed me like I was a treat. I'm sure she only did that because she was warming me up, making my blood sweeter, like the fermentation process with grapes. I've learned vampires like the taste of a sexually aroused human's blood. Hell, I was inside her when she bit me. Had she worked me up enough to give herself a toothache? Because dammit, if my teeth aren't clenching now from the thought of that bite...

God, that bite. When her fangs impacted me, I came again, harder than the first time. Just the thought of her fangs grazing my neck has my dick jumping.

What in the hell is wrong with me? Am I forgetting what she is? She is a monster who took a piece out of me.

Except, this time, I liked it. I got off on it. I want to turn the car around and have her bite me again.

At a stop sign, I reach for my neck. The twin puncture marks throb as I graze them. There is no pain. With only a slight touch, my body shudders as it remembers the feel of her lips on my skin. I shiver at the memory of how her throat worked to pull my blood from me. My dick throbs in my pants, wanting in on the action.

That did not happen the first time with that nightmare, Domitia. That wound still smarts from when she ripped my flesh. When I touch it now, my passion for Sanai cools.

But not entirely. Her taste is still on my tongue. The vision of her laid out before me as an offering will never leave my mind.

Why didn't she take these thoughts of her, these memories of us, from my mind? Is that her play? To leave me wanting more of her?

I yank the video pin from my shirt. I have the evidence in my hands to expose this world to all of humanity. To expose her. To have her hunted.

The thought of any pain coming to Sanai makes my gut sicken. The thought of anyone seeing her body exposed makes me rage.

I drop the pin. It clatters to the floor of the car. I give it my heel, twisting the circuitry for good measure.

I pull out my phone and call up the app. My finger hovers over the delete key for the stream. My thumb feels heavy as I press it. Somehow, instead of the delete key, I manage to hit play.

Sanai's face comes into view. Her smile is

appraising as she comes closer to the camera. Her gaze dips up and down, her brows lifting as though they like what she sees.

"You work for Frangelico?" Those are my words, the first I said to her.

"No," comes that sultry voice that makes my skin tingle. "I work for no man."

I'm sitting in the middle of the street, out in the middle of wine country. Instead of putting my car in park, my foot stays on the brake. My thumb stays away from the delete button as I watch the entire scene between me and Sanai play out.

"You're not what I expected," she says.

I can only see her face in the video—fitting, as she came up to my chest. Her gaze constantly roams up and down my body. A few times, she licks those lush lips. But as hard as I stare at her, I don't see carnivorous hunger. Only carnal.

She said I wasn't what she expected. She was not what I expected. I had gone into that club to take the supernatural world down. In truth, Sanai brought me to my knees with just a smile.

I was on my knees at this point in the video. The only view I got was of the floor. But I hear her cries of pleasure as my tongue worked to master her. I catch sight of her foot tethered to the post of the massage table. The sight of the twine crisscrossing her trim ankles makes my dick pulse.

"I'll be good," she says. "I'll hold still."

That's what I truly wanted, for her to hold still while I tasted every inch of her skin. For her to behave as I fucked her senseless. For her to be bound to me for the rest of our lives.

And then I hear myself calling her a monster.

The camera catches her face as her regal features fall. Her lip trembles before it stiffens. Her throat works before that elegant column lengthens. And then she is gone.

She didn't attack me. She didn't walk away from me. I'd left her. And I have no idea how to find her again.

I lift my foot from the brake. The car rolls forward. With a tap of the gas pedal, I am back in motion.

My car stops in front of the Serrano vineyard. I had been heading home, but I feel the need to be around family.

The door at the front of the Serrano manse isn't locked. Why would it be? The males inside would scent any danger as it came into the gate. They could rip out the throat of any threat.

When I walk inside, I find both men with their

arms wrapped around my sisters. Cari is curled in Hadrian's lap, her head resting on his heart. Marechal sits next to Gaius, her head leaning against his shoulder.

On the television is the old black and white family sitcom, *The Munsters*: the show where Frankenstein's monster and his vampire bride live in a suburbia that struggles to accept them.

"Arnie, you came."

"Ouch," I grunt as I'm nearly crushed when Cari embraces me.

"Careful, Carignan," warns Hadrian. "Unless you want to break your brother."

"Sorry, Arnie," Cari says as she pulls away. "I don't know my own strength."

My baby sister smiles at me. It's the same goofy grin she wore as a child. She looks the same, except instead of a gap-toothed grin, she has fangs.

I wait for the fear to arise. It doesn't come. Only the fraternal love I've had for my sister since I watched her take her first steps.

I pull Cari back to me. This time it's Cari who protests as I hug her tightly.

"You okay?" asks Marechal, rubbing me on the shoulder. "Rough day at work?"

"Yeah," I say, as I reach out to include her in the embrace.

"Didn't get everything checked off your list?" Marechal asks.

"No, I accomplished what I set out to do." I let my sisters go and scratch at the ache in my chest. "There were just... unintended consequences."

"Uh oh," says Cari, returning to Hadrian's lap. "You should know my brother does not like surprises. He likes things to go exactly as planned."

Hadrian smiles at his bride, looking at her like she is both the star he wished on, and wished for. Only a couple of weeks ago, I determined that Hadrian has an unhealthy obsession with my sister. I see it clearly tonight. That is the look of a man hopelessly in love.

"Anything we can help with?" asks Gaius as Marechal comes back beside him.

I chuckle at the offer. I'm not sure which would be the funnier ask. Should I tell Gaius about my intent to expose his kind to the world? Or should I regale him with the account of my misstep of falling for one of his kind and then calling her a monster, thereby ensuring she will have nothing to do with me, ever?

"You're family now," Gaius is saying. "I know

we're not the brothers you would've liked, but we're the brothers you've got, and we take care of our own."

He's right. This is my family now. A collection of munsters trying to fit into the world we all find ourselves in.

The theme song to the sitcom plays through the television set, signaling the end of the show. There is a knot in my stomach. A dull heaviness in my chest.

"Why don't you get some rest?" says Gaius. "Whatever it is, we can talk about it tomorrow night."

He doesn't need to compel me to take that direction. I go to the guest room Gaius indicates. My eyes are closed before my head hits the pillow. But even before my lids shut, all I can see is her face.

Deleting the video saved her and my family from a world that would struggle to accept them. But I have to face facts. Sanai's face will play on a loop in my mind for the rest of my life. If I don't find her and make things right, the color will drain from my world.

12

———

"**Y**ou're still in bed? It's nine at night. You're usually up by the first moonbeam."

I turn away from the moonlight that enters the room as Fay spreads the curtains. I'm not ready to greet this new night. I don't know when I'll be ready to greet any other night.

"You've already missed the first meal. The queen gave the eunuchs honeyed wine, and I have to say I like the sugary taste of the meal."

The thought of another male's blood makes my

stomach churn. Fay thinks blood tinged with wine is sweet to the tongue. If she has a sip from a virile male, she'll be incapacitated with one draw. A male high on the endorphins of sex would send her walking into the sunlight for a dust bath.

"What's gotten into you?" Fay sits on the edge of the bed. Her slight form barely causes a dip in the mattress.

Her question is a loaded one. Little does she know, something has definitely gotten into me. More like someone.

I can still feel Arneis everywhere. On my tongue, between my thighs, and worse... in my heart.

"I'm just tired, Fayola. I think I'll rest for the day while you and the queen go to the Serranos' meeting."

Staying in bed will also give me an excuse to not see the queen. Sooner or later, she will hear of my dealings at Club Toxic last night. Will she cast me out? And for which transgression? Attempting to take the meeting with the Serranos? Exposing the supernatural world to humans? Or having a sexual encounter with a man?

Whatever punishment she metes out to me, I will take it, even though I have already learned the error of my ways. Queen Malika was right to keep us from the vile creatures known as man. One brought me to such heights of pleasure, only to dash me down into unimaginable pain.

I know now why the queen cuts off that appendage of any man who wants to remain in her presence. She has only been trying to protect herself and her daughters from men's treachery.

I wonder if the queen has ever had her own intimate encounters with men. If she had had a night like mine, she certainly wouldn't have cut off Arneis's member. Even though his words after the act had cut deep, the way he'd kissed my body and moved inside of me had been magic.

"Well, you're going to have to rally," Fay says, rising from the bed. "The queen mother is looking for you."

I let out a long and weary sigh. It's time to face the drums.

So, he's done it. Part of me hadn't believed he truly would: that he would expose not just my fangs, but my body to the world. He'd put on display what we shared between us like it meant nothing. Likely because it hadn't meant anything to him.

I dress in a colorful bazin. The vibrant cloth is a trademark of my mother's people, from the western part of the African continent. I pull on the cowrie shell necklace that was an heirloom from Queen Amina, the warrior regent and my great, great grandmother. If I am going to be chastised or cast out, it will be with my head held high like my fearless ancestor.

When I walk into the room where the queen is, I see that she is feeding. Queen Malika's braids fall forward, obscuring her face as her fangs sink into the neck of the man on his knees. The man's face is docile as she takes her meal. His hands are clasped in front of him in his lap, where his member would lie if he still had it attached.

But there is pleasure on his features. I know that a vampire's bite can be enjoyable to humans. However, I suspect the gratification on this man's face has more to do with serving his queen than sexual stimulation.

When I bit into Arneis's jugular, he groaned with pleasure. I knew it was pleasure because I felt his cock pressing into me and spending.

Queen Malika unlatches from the blood servant's neck, and the man sags. Am I imagining things, or did his eyes flutter? He keeps his eyes closed, his features going docile once more.

The queen dabs at her mouth with a cloth. "Good evening, *hartlam*. Have you eaten?"

Hartlam? Eaten? Where is the ire, the anger over what I've cost the race of vampires the world over?

"You'll need to hurry," the queen says. "We're leaving in a quarter-hour."

"Leaving?"

So this is it. She's sending me back across the ocean. Even if I had wanted to search for Arneis, I won't be able to. I will truly never see him again.

"Yes," says the queen. "Our meeting with the Serranos is in an hour. There's an awful belief about the Africans who were stolen from the motherland and brought here. The notion is that they are always late to functions. They call it *CP time*. I don't know what it stands for but it's such an erroneous way to think when my ancestors first broke the day into time periods using obelisks."

I ignore the history lesson and focus on the earlier words. "You want me to come with you to the Serranos meeting?"

"Yes, *hartlam*. I think you were right. It's time you take on more responsibilities."

My tongue is tied. I'm not busted. I haven't been exposed.

Here I am, getting what I wanted after doing exactly what I wasn't supposed to be doing. And I am being rewarded for it. But all I can think is not about how to extend our financial empire. All I can think is: will I see Arneis at the Serranos'?

13

____

Arneis

"Please."

The fabric of her colorful gown inches up her lithe thighs. Her caramel against my honeyed skin tones makes my mouth water, but not as much as watching the rope bind her legs.

"Please."

I pull the rope tight. The twine pinches her skin, holding her tight. My fingers ache to hold her flesh in mine again.

"Hold still," I hear myself say. "I want to remember every detail of this moment."

I can't see the deep pink of her intimate flesh as I

move closer. But I remember every detail. Every taste. Every scent. Every quiver.

The sound of Sanai's cries fills my ears until she cries out. Darkness still colors the screen on my phone as the camera's eye presses against the massage table. Even though she has orgasmed, I haven't had my fill. I lap at the nectar that seeps from her core. The sound of my tongue against her flesh is the chorus to the whimpers of her voice.

It's over all too quickly. I press rewind and listen to the scene again. And then again, making sure to stop before the end, when I became a monster to the precious creature who'd allowed me so close to her treasure.

I barely slept a wink all last night and into the day. My thoughts were consumed with Sanai.

My hand goes to my neck. It seeks her bite. The small puckers make my whole body sizzle with want when I touch them. It's a want that will never be filled, because I will never see her again. Except in my mind and on this video. So I stay in bed and allow myself to get lost in her as the day goes by.

"Arneis, get up," calls Cari from the other side of the locked door.

My thumb scrambles to pause the video before Sanai can scream her orgasm again.

"We're making pancakes."

I sit up in the bed. I wasn't aware that vampires ate. My stomach grumbles, reminding me that I haven't eaten in over twenty-four hours. I throw water on my face, then put on a clean shirt left by Gaius. The two of us are the same size, and with similar tastes in clothing, though this garment likely costs the same amount as my annual salary as a public servant.

Making my way into the kitchens, I see that a feast is laid out on the tables. My sisters are flipping flapjacks onto a serving plate. Gaius is sliding crepes onto a platter. Hadrian mixes up sangria in a glass pitcher.

I sit down and allow my older sister to fuss over me. Marechal fusses over all attended, as is her way. I am surprised that she is here and not back in her lab, blending the latest grapes from the harvest. She worked impossible hours before. Much like I did. But here we are, sitting down for a family dinner—or first meal, as it is called in this household.

I can't follow the train of conversation. Much of it has to do with Virius, the third Serrano brother, who was recently taken hostage by a group of female shifters—women who had worked the harvest on the Durand vineyards for as long as I can remember.

No one at the table seems overly concerned about Virius's predicament. I was there the night he was taken. It seemed to me that the male wanted to be kidnapped by the voluptuous leader of the jaguar shifters.

"We'll get this cleaned up before your guests get here," says Cari.

"Don't bother," says Hadrian, pulling her into his embrace. "We'll take care of it. You two enjoy your girls' night out."

"Cari and I are headed out for some shopping and girl time," says Marechal. "Do you want to come, Arnie?"

"To girl time? No, thank you."

Spending time with my sisters has always been a favorite pastime of mine. Except when they go shopping. I tend to frequent the same stores. When I do, I go in, get exactly what I want, and head out. Marechal and Cari have to try on different versions of the same clothing in various stores, all of which easily takes hours.

Before they head out, my sisters both embrace me. Then they're taken back into the arms of their vampire lovers. I watch silently as Hadrian and

Gaius fuss over them before reluctantly letting them climb into Cari's car.

"They have you two wrapped around their fingers," I say out loud.

"True," says Hadrian. "My still heart beats for that woman."

"Marechal consumes my waking thoughts," says Gaius. "My sleeping ones, too."

Hadrian pulls out his phone. I can see he has a tracking app open. The bleeping dot moves down the street in front of us. He sees me staring and shrugs. "I'm open about my obsession with her."

For the first time since I've known the man, I crack a smile. These two truly love my sisters. They would never let anything bad happen to them. I have never felt as deeply as they do for any of my girlfriends.

I scratch at the back of my head. My hand grazes over one of the bumps of my neck, the one that pains me. Hadrian catches my movements.

"Domitia was cruel," he says. "We are not all like her. Many of us live in close-knit families and make our way through life together. But there are some who are power-hungry and sadistic. Just as you would find in humanity."

I'm coming to see that. My hand tracks over to my other bite. A different shudder runs through me.

"You have a second bite," says Hadrian. "Exactly where were you last night?"

I don't answer, though I know that I will have to in order to get their help in finding Sanai. I'm just not sure where to begin.

"I got a bill from Club Toxic this evening," says Gaius. "It was for a private room. But I was here at home all night."

That's as good a place as any to start. But before I can open my mouth, a car pulls up in the drive. It's not Cari's car. This is a luxurious town car, with tinted windows.

I know who will step out of it before I see her. I'm already moving towards her. My heartbeat kicks up. My thoughts are consumed with her.

And then I see her.

14

Sanai

I like this part of the desert state better. It brings to mind the rolling vineyards in northern Africa. Even though it's the dark of night, I can make out some vibrant colors in the wine country. The smell of Carignan berries tickles my nose. My tongue detects the sweetness of Marechal grapes nearby. The two scents together rouse my hunger, making me think of Arneis.

His blood tasted of the sweetness I now smell. Was he brought up in wine country? He said he is related to the Serranos. Those three brothers trade in wine. It's why the queen and I are going to see them: to expand the wine trade from our vineyards in Algeria, Morocco, and Tunisia.

"You're different."

I turn to the Queen Mother. She is eyeing me with those shrewd eyes. I'm not sure what she sees. The fact that my sacred berry has been plucked?

"You seem more sedate. Perhaps even more mature."

I purse my lips instead of responding. I don't want her to know that the reason for my overnight growth spurt is a man. Or do I want her to know it? I loved everything that happened between Arneis and myself. Everything up until the end.

"When we go home, I'm giving you more responsibility."

Home? To an enclosed palace and eunuchs, where I have to keep my legs closed and my mouth shut about the advancements in the world? Is that the life I want?

The answer is clear in my mind. It rings loudly in my ears. I can't go back. I want to stay here in this monochrome city, where there lives a man with eyes the same color as the grapes in the vineyard outside the window.

"What if I stay here?" I say. "It will be inconvenient to travel across the ocean each time we need to have a meeting or deal in a transaction."

"You expect me to throw one of my daughters to the wolves?" The corners of the queen's mouth turn down.

"Your daughter is a vampire, and has your blood. A dog would heel under my command."

Queen Malika grins at this. Her chin lifts and her chest thrusts out as she regarded me.

I mirror her movements. I love this woman. I have looked up to her for so many years for all she's done for my people, for my family, and for me personally.

But I come to a realization then—one just as big as losing both my virginity and my heart to a man who hates my kind. Just like I am not the demoness who hurt Arneis, I am not my queen. And I do not want to be her.

I open my mouth to tell her this, but the car comes to a halt. I hear the crunch of tires underfoot. I feel the world stop around me. I smell him before I see him.

Somewhere in the back of my mind, I knew there was a possibility that he might be here. His features had faltered when he'd called me a monster, as though he'd had trouble making the falsehood stick in his mind. As he looks at me now, I know he doesn't see something from his nightmares.

Arneis walks out of the front door of the impressive house, a palace in its own right. He is flanked by two large males. But my gaze keeps going back to him.

Shame colors his dark eyes. The purse of his lips begs me for my forgiveness. I give him my hand.

"Princess Sanai Amina Mohamud of the queendom of Orun. It's a pleasure to make your acquaintance."

Arneis takes my hand in his. He doesn't bow over it and kiss my knuckles as he should. Instead, he stares deeply into my eyes, trying to communicate a depth of feeling that only I can understand. Or so I think.

"What is the meaning of this?" asks the queen.

"Your Majesty." The other two men step forward. "Gaius Serrano at your service. This is my brother, Hadrian."

Queen Malika waves away the other two vampires. "Why is there a human touching my daughter? Do you not have control over your servants?"

"Arneis is our brother," says Hadrian.

"He's also a leader in the human community,"

says Gaius. "You'll need his help if you intend to distribute your wine here."

The queen sneers. She never deals directly with humans, especially if said human is a man who is fully intact. If she even dares glance at Arneis's manhood, she'll have to regenerate her hand, because I will have clawed it off.

She looks between me and Arneis, her regal scowl firmly in place. But in the end, she inclines her head, the highest of praise a human could hope to receive from her. With a swish of her skirts, Queen Malika steps past Arneis and me as we are welcomed into the Serrano home.

"Forgive me," Arneis says once we are alone. "For what I said to you. It's not what's in my heart."

"I'll forgive you if you'll forgive me for the bite."

"No," he says. "Never."

My heart sinks. I make to shrink away from him, but I can't. He's holding onto my hand. His grip tightens when I try to pull away.

"It was your bite that woke me up," he says. "It made me see the error of my ways. I thought I hated your kind. I thought vampires had stolen something from me. But I was wrong. Coming into this world has brought me to you."

A slow grin spreads across my face. He wants me. I can have him.

Arneis dips his head to mine, but before our lips can connect—

"Sanai!"

I groan. Arneis presses his thumb to my lips. I kiss it, then nick it for good measure. His breath catches as I suck the drop of blood away.

That was just an appetizer. I plan to sink my claws into this man as soon as possible. For now, we walk slowly towards the open door.

15

Arneis

The talks last an hour. It's fifty-five minutes longer than I cared to speak. By the sixtieth minute, I'm raring to get my hands on the ties of Sanai's dress.

Today, she wears another vibrantly colored gown. Reds and blues and yellows crisscross her slender form in strategically placed strips. Just a few flicks of my fingers, and I could have her hands bound over her head, leaving the rest of her free to slake my desires. I try to push my carnal thoughts aside and pay attention to the lecture at hand. But the only thing I can focus on is how I will bring Sanai to pleasure after this talk is over.

As beautiful as she is, Sanai is just as brilliant. When it comes to the wine trade, she is knowledgeable and a slick negotiator. I concede on all of her demands. Not only because I have fallen in love with this woman. I concede because her business in Tucson will be a boon to the citizens here.

By the end of the negotiations, I've made a decision. I will be leaving public life. Tomorrow, I will put away my campaign signs and all of my dreams for higher office. I can't have my personal life scrutinized if I plan to spend the rest of my nights with a vampire.

"It's time for us to go," says Queen Malika.

The woman rises, but Sanai remains seated. "I'm staying."

"That was still up for discussion, child."

I find it fascinating that the queen calls Sanai a child even though the queen looks far younger. I am sure the monarch is centuries old. Maybe even millennia. Which brings me to wonder, exactly how old is the woman I want to hitch my life to?

"I'll find my own way from here, Your Majesty." Sanai's tone is firm, much like when we were negotiating the terms of distributing her queendom's wines here.

Something passes between the women. The queen looks between her daughter and me. I prepare to speak up, to let her know that I will protect Sanai with everything in me. But Sanai beats me to it.

"Don't worry, my queen. I have him wrapped around my finger. The queendom's interest will flourish here, you have my word."

After another long moment, Queen Malika gives a curt nod of her head. Sanai rises and rushes into her arms. The queen takes the embrace stiffly. But I see the crease of worry in her brow, much like the one I always get when my sisters are too long out of my sight.

When the queen is gone, I look up to note that Gaius and Hadrian have made their own exits. It's just me and the princess.

"Listen, Sanai. Let me explain—"

She is on me before I can get another word out. She claims my mouth with her own, pressing the words into my lips. "Explain later. Love me now."

This meeting has finally taken the turn I was hoping for. "I move that we take this to the bedroom."

"I second that motion."

I tug Sanai to the bedroom I slept in the night before. Before I've even closed the door, she's kicked off her shoes and is moving the straps of her dress down her body.

"No," I say. "Let me."

I didn't get to see her completely naked last night. We'd simply moved enough of our clothing out of the way to get at each other. Now, and for the rest of our lives, I plan to savor every second, every inch of flesh.

I slip the gown down Sanai's shoulders. The mounds of her breasts appear like summits I've worked hard to reach. I bend down and take the cocoa-dusted nipples into my mouth.

Sanai lets out a hungry moan at my tongue's first brush. I want to let her know that I'm going to feed her lust. I'm going to feed all of her appetites. But first, I need her to hold still.

With the gown at her midsection, I use the ropes to twine the fabric about her forearms. Sanai gasps, but she holds still for me. When I look up into her face, I see that her gaze is wide with want.

When I'm done, I take a step back from her. She stands where I left her. Her perky breasts sit high on her chest. Her elegant arms are bound to her stomach by the cords that had held up her dress. The bottom half of the dress is pooled at her feet, giving me access to the shadowed V between her thighs.

She presses her thighs together. I can hear the slickness gathered there. I can scent her readiness.

I peel off my clothing, not taking my eyes off her as I do so. "On the bed."

Sanai grins at my command, and does as she's told and climbs onto the mattress.

"Spread your thighs."

Again, she follows my orders. With her knees splayed wide, I slide beneath her torso to reward her obedience. When my tongue touches her sex, she throws her head back.

I latch my mouth around her sex, taking in the sweetness that's more vibrant than any grape I've harvested. Reaching my hands up, I steady her hips, locking her into place over me as I drink her down. Without the use of her arms to balance herself, Sanai is near to keeling over with the long laps I'm taking to her folds.

She rocks her hips against my tongue, faster and faster, getting wetter and wetter with each gyration. Back and forth her hips go, round and round and from side to side. She is dancing on my mouth. I spin my tongue around her clit, dipping in and out of her core until we are both dizzy.

When she comes down from her orgasm, I lift her hips and place her in my lap. Her slick core is greeted by my hard cock. As I slide inside her, I feel the aftershocks of her orgasm grabbing onto me for purchase.

Sanai opens pleasure-drunk eyes to gaze up at me. Her hands are between our chests, her fingernails scraping against my heart. I catch her gaze as it slips to the side of my neck where the veins there pulse with eagerness. As though it is hungry for her bite.

"Do it," I say.

Her breath quickens. Her fingers curl. Her eyes flare wider. Then they narrow as she searches my gaze.

"I'm inside of you," I say. "I want you inside of me."

Her soft sigh makes my chest puff up with what I know is love. Her fingers brush the side of my mouth in a gentle caress that nearly breaks me. Her eyes soften, and reflect back the love that has blossomed in my heart.

Sanai turns from the bite she gave me last night. Instead, she moves to the other side of my neck, where the first bite is. She kisses down my chin until she reaches the spot that has given me nightmares.

When her teeth strike that spot, my balls tighten. When her lips fasten to my flesh, I pull her hips flush against me. When she pulls my life's essence from me, I release my seed into her.

Somewhere in the house, a clock chimes the new hour. Sanai and I have reached the end of this meeting's agenda. With both our bodies spent, there is no more business to conduct this night. With our hearts beating as one, our breaths in sync, and our limbs entwined, we close our eyes and declare the business between us adjourned... until our next regularly scheduled meeting. Which will take place tomorrow night, and then again the next night. For the rest of our lives.

THE VALKYRIE'S CLAIM

A LAST DRAGONS NOVELLA

INES JOHNSON

CHAPTER 1

"Oh, yes, yes, Big Daddy. You're the best I've ever had."

Regin took a sip of her soda pop. The fizzy drink tickled her nose causing her to wiggle it, much like the woman's torso was doing at the moment. Regin slunk back in the shadows of the window, not wanting to detract from the woman's performance. Because it was a performance. Regin knew a lie when she heard one.

"You're so big, Big Daddy. You're going to split me right open."

That wasn't likely. Big Daddy was better known as Joey "The Whale" Amato because he made men swim with the fishes. Joey was as big as a whale. His cheeks were fat and made his head look like an overinflated balloon. His belly was so round both on the sides and in the front that the flesh fell over his waistline.

Unfortunately, The Whale wasn't big in all the right places. Regin had caught sight of his member before it disappeared inside the bouncing liar. The only thing that little extension would split would've been her gut with laughter.

Regin took another swig of her fizzy drink. Cola was the best part of visiting this side of the Veil. It was a sweet sort of ale that had none of the side effects of lethargy or stupidness. Though not much affected her as one of the daughters of the Goddess. Yet somehow the fizzy drink put a pep in her step.

Regin was lounging while she waited for this little act to finish. She'd parked her ride outside the window of her prey while she knocked back her first cold one. Once this party was over Big Daddy Whale was on his way to Hell for his crimes against humanity.

Mother didn't mind a few bad deeds now and then. But She drew the line at serial murders. That was the realm of the gods with plagues and floods and dysentery. Joey had taken out enough of Mother's pets to equal a small town. It was time for his comeuppance.

However, Regin was being polite, using the manners neither of her parents taught her, and letting The Whale blow his load one more time before eternal damnation. She was cool like that. She knew the sexual act could take a while and she had a whole other bottle of soda to get to so she-

"Oh, oh, ohhhhh," groaned The Whale.

Joey's flabby flesh stiffened where it could. His flat butt cheeks clenched as he lifted them off the bed with effort. His mouth gaped open, like a dead fish, and his eyes squeezed shut.

It was over already? Regin had only had two sips of her first soda.

Staring over his shoulder, the little actress rolled her eyes but continued her moaning praise. "Oh, Big Daddy. No one's ever made me feel like that before. You are a Golden God."

Regin doubted Thor, the actual Golden God, would appreciate the comparison. His exploits in Asgard were the stuff of legends.

She was lucky she hadn't been born a human female. Men were some of the dumbest creatures she'd ever encountered. She would've counted human females as intelligent, except somehow they'd let males have power over them.

Was it because of the sex? Were men's wangs

truly that magical? They didn't look like anything special to Regin. She'd likely have a better time digging up worms from the earth. At least they could regenerate when you cut off the head.

Male bodies were so jiggly and hairy and smelly. She truly didn't see the draw. But it was not her lot in life to see the draw. She was here to collect.

Regin waited for the female to collect her clothes, collect her payment, and then abscond from the room. She didn't need an audience for her performance. Once the door shut behind the woman it was showtime.

Stepping over the ledge of the window, Regin launched inside the room. She tucked and rolled over the shag carpet. When she was at the foot of the bed, she brandished her swords.

It was a pointless demonstration of her prowess. The Whale was snoring. His large belly rising and falling. His tiny member shriveled up smaller than a worm.

How could women stomach the touch of a male, much less their thrusting?

Regin poked the man with the blunt end of her sword. She was afraid that poking him with the pointy end would make him burst like a balloon and she'd be left with innards to take back home.

It took a couple more pokes before Joey woke up. He came to with a cough and sputter. Some of his dribble got on Regin's armor. Great.

"Here for round two, sweetheart?" he asked.

Gross. Besides, Regin doubted he could even mount an offense for round two. His eyes widened when he saw that there wasn't a naked woman in front of him, but a woman in full armor with a sword come to service him.

"Who sent you? Whoever it is, I'll have their heads and yours, you dumb broad."

In response, Regin flipped him over and hogtied him.

"You can't do this. Do you know who I am?"

He screamed like a little girl when she tossed him out the window. He landed on her dragon's back and promptly peed himself.

The Big Daddy Whale kept his protests, pleas, and propositions up all the way to the Veil; the rip in the fabric of the earth where the Goddess tinkered on Her creations. Humans once called this place the Garden of Eden, back when they were residents.

By the time they got to Shepard's Town, Regin had a raging headache and was contemplating stopping into God's Teet for a pint. She landed her dragon behind the bar and began to dismount when she realized she wasn't the only one who was looking forward to a tall glass of spirits.

"Oh, yes, yes, Big Dragon. You're the best I've ever had."

A fairy's lithe legs were wrapped around the tight backside of a male whose physique would've given the Golden God a run for his money. There were no rolls on this male's body. Unless you counted the muscles of his arms and thighs.

"You're so big, Draco. You're going to split me right open."

Though the reality of the fairy's words was unlikely, because a fairy was mostly sinew and fluids with no bones, the sentiment was true. Regin caught glimpses of Draco's size as he slipped in and out of the fairy's most private of places. His whole member didn't sink inside her pink sheath.

Regin had heard of the dragon shifter, Draco. Many fairies whispered his name in the town. And they each did it with a covetous sigh.

Draco was the reason Regin had wondered about the sexual act in the first place. What, she wondered, could make a female tremble with just a mention of a male's name? Well, she was seeing the reason with her own eyes.

Draco swiveled his hips as he thrust. The fairy

threw her head back in wild abandon. He caught her wrists in one hand and stretched them over her head, trapping her against him as he continued his wanton assault.

They were screwing up against the side of the bar. He pounded into her like a hammer would a nail. With such a ruckus Regin was sure everyone inside God's Teet could hear them.

If he was worried about an audience, Draco gave no indication. He increased his speed, pounding into the fairy with a *thump thump thump*. Soon her legs began to tremble, shaking like a leaf at the edge of a branch.

Draco slipped his finger between them. Regin could see his hand moving in a circular motion in time to his thumps. Within seconds, the fairy threw her head back and screamed.

But it wasn't a scream of pain. Not exactly. It was as though the pain was so exquisite that the fairy had to let some of the intensity out.

Regin gulped at the sight and sound of it. She felt her mouth-watering. She felt heat in the space between her thighs. A heat that she didn't know could turn up there.

Her mind filled with want. Her throat was dry from thirst. Her fingers clenched with need.

And then Draco's gaze snapped up and locked on her.

Regin felt she should run. But she was a Valkyrie. She was a daughter of the Goddess. She ran from nothing. Yet the sounds of feet hitting pavement were plain in her ears.

Still thrusting, Draco's gaze flicked past her. His green eyes widened and then narrowed as though sensing prey.

With difficulty, Regin tore her gaze away from the dragon. Running away in the dark she saw the flab of giant, human whale. Joey was getting away. All because she had been peeping at a male waving his magical wang.

Ugh, men.

CHAPTER 2

Draco switched his gaze from the woman watching him fuck Gardenia to the fat man running away in the dark of the night. He couldn't help but think that that man could've been him.

Not with all that flesh, of course. Dragon shifters were too well-crafted to carry excess weight. The fat would impede flying. Come to think of it, fairies were always lean. Was the man a troll? In Shephard's Town?

In any case, the runaway troll, with a leaner build and better hair, could've have been Draco. He was running away from his problems, too. Although if Draco had a woman like the one watching him screw Gardenia after him, he didn't think he'd run so fast.

She was tall and tone. With golden hair that looked like strands of sun. She was covered from head to toe in a blueish cloth. And there were... were those swords on her hips?

Fuck. No. Oh no, no. She was a Valkyrie.

What was a Valkyrie doing watching him fuck? Everyone knew the female warriors were asexual, or not sexual at all. Yet she had her gaze fixed on him. And fuck, he was still fucking Gardenia. Because for a second there, after he'd caught sight of the blonde in the dark, he'd imagined he was fucking her instead.

But that was insanity. It could never happen. She was a fucking Valkyrie.

Draco pulled out of Gardenia's warm heat. It wasn't a hardship to do so. The fairy had already climaxed for the third time, or fourth? He'd lost count.

He hadn't gotten off himself. He hadn't been close. Not until he'd seen the blonde in the shadows. But the retraction of his balls wasn't a bad thing. He knew that blowing his load would only satisfy him for a few moments before he was restless again. Might as well be restless with blue balls than have his balls cut off by a Valkyrie's sword.

Gardenia crumpled into a heap at his feet once he took her from his still hard cock.

The Valkyrie's back was to him now. She was watching the large male run off into the forest. So, he wasn't a troll at all. He was a human male, which was far worse.

"Look what you made me do," the Valkyrie growled. Her eyes were golden bright, like a cat's. Her pointed ears were erect and alert.

Him? Draco hadn't told her to look at him. But he wasn't about to argue with a Valkyrie. Even though his life sucked at the moment, there was still some value in it.

The Valkyrie stomped off behind the running man. Draco yanked up his pants and took off after the Valkyrie. She wasn't hard to catch up with. She didn't run after her quarry.

Why would she? Valkyrie always caught their prey. So why was he following behind her? What was he going to do? Help?

Like she needed it. She'd likely turn on him and run him through with her sword.

Maybe that's what he wanted? Instead of sticking his sword in a willing fairy, maybe he yearned to be run through and end his miserable existence?

"There," said Draco. The bushes had rumbled and he caught sight of pasty flesh.

"Do you think I can't scent my prey," the Valkyrie tossed over her shoulder.

Her feet struck the ground in a steady rhythm drawing Draco's eyes to her thigh-high boots. Even though he was a dragon, and the highest on the food chain in the Veil when it came to shifters, he'd been taught to avert his gaze from Valkyrie. The females were beyond the hierarchy of beasts roaming these lands.

Still, Draco had always had a thing about long legs encased in leather that ended in heels. He was so entranced by her boots that he walked right into her back causing her to trip.

He held out his hands to steady her but was met with a blade at his throat.

"I'm sorry," he said. "I was just trying to-"

"Help?" Her perfectly shaped lips puckered at the end of the word. "I don't need your help. Go back to poking your fairy."

Draco should've turned on his heel then. But he didn't. His steps fell in line behind hers.

Yes, he must have a death wish. Or maybe he just wanted to be a help to one female tonight instead of sending her off to her death.

"I'll cut him off at the back," said Draco. "Corner him, so he can't escape."

"There's no way he could escape," she said. "He's in the Veil."

Her words were true. But still, Draco went the long way around. His dragon gave him his wings and he sailed to the other side of the woods. Once there, he heard a rustle in the leaves.

Had she already caught him? That was unlikely. She was walking at a steady clip. She hadn't likely arrived yet. But Draco didn't want the man getting away. A loose human male would be a nuisance in the Veil.

Draco jumped out of his hiding place. Once again, he narrowly missed the sharp end of the Valkyrie's blade. Only this time they both were unsteady on their feet.

Down they went, tumbling sideways, ass over belly. He landed with a thud on his back with her over top of him. Her knees were spread on either side of his hips. His cock, which had been erect, went harder than stone as it nestled between her thighs.

The blade at his throat did nothing to lower that mast. In fact, the sharp edge turned him on more. He definitely had a death wish.

"What are you doing?" she demanded. But her words were breathy. Was there a wanton note to them?

No. He had to be imagining that.

The other things he was imagining? What her lips would taste like. How tight and warm her unbreached core would be. What sounds she'd make as he threw her thighs over his shoulders and thrust inside her until his balls slapped her tight ass. While she wore those boots.

Her nostrils flared as though she could hear his thoughts. She might be able to. She was a daughter of the Goddess.

Her gaze dipped to his lips. Her hands were on his chest. Did she just grope his peck a little bit? Had her hips lowered a fraction? Was she now sitting directly on his erection? Did her hips swivel just slightly over the bulge in his pants?

Should he...? He was already at death's door. Why not. Draco tilted his hips up to meet the warm V between her thighs.

She gasped. It was only a slight inhale, but he heard it. By the Goddess, she wanted him.

"Ouch."

Draco reached up to his neck. His fingers came away bloody. When he looked up she was gone.

In the distance, he heard the squeal of a little girl. Oh, no. That had to be the fat man she'd gone after. She'd captured him and it was all over. She would be gone, flying to deposit the man into the bowels of Valhalla. He was lucky he wasn't being thrown over the back of a feral dragon and facing the same fate for the liberty he'd taken with her.

Draco lay in the grass for long moments after her scent faded. His fingers pressed against the blood trickling down from where her blade had kissed his flesh. His dick still throbbed from the contact of her heat.

He hadn't even breached her inner walls and yet he felt a sense of completion. Not a single one of his worries troubled him as he lay wrapped in the memory of her touch. And it lasted, for longer than a few moments. It lasted until the sun came up on a new day.

CHAPTER 3

Regin tossed the trash inside the door. The male bodies inside backed up and stepped aside to make way for the newest bit of refuse. Joey The Whale slipped on his bloodied feet and tumbled down on his bare ass.

"Please," he said to Regin. "I'll pay you whatever you want."

"With what?" she said. "All you have left in the world that belongs to you is your seed. And no one here has any interest in that."

Joey looked down at his shriveled manhood. The limp member didn't look as though it would give any essence anytime soon. Especially not when he was surrounded by thousands of other males.

The latest addition to Valhalla looked up at his

cellmates. The first to make his way over was a greasy black-haired, mustached man. Followed by a similarly-colored man, but only a foot shorter. Their names were Napoléon Bonaparte and Adolph Hitler. Léon and Dolph always called dibstones on any pale-skinned man that entered the doors of Hell.

But it looked like they'd have a fight on their hands. Genghis Khan had his beady eyes on Joey, too. It would be a bloody battle.

Regin shut and locked the door. After the snick of the gear, the screams died down until they were less than a whisper.

Walking away from the massive doorway, she loosened her breastplates. The armor came away leaving her breasts feeling both tender and heavy. Her nipples had swollen to sharp points during the heat of the battle to retrieve her quarry, and they hadn't softened since.

She pulled off her leg coverings. For some reason her thighs were unsteady. They even shook a bit, like a newborn foal's.

And then there was her head. The sensation she felt wasn't the throbbing ache of a megrim. Something pulsed at the forefront of her brain, but when she closed her eyes to try and relieve some of the pressure, all she saw was him.

Draco's thrusting hips. His clenching buttocks. The muscles of his back moving and reshaping under the power of his movements. But he wasn't thrusting into the core of a fairy any longer.

Gone were the willowy limbs of a fae. In their place were creamy white thighs. A thatch of golden fuzz mingling with the dark of Draco's groin. His fingers were there on that golden core, brushing aside the light curls and finding a swollen pink nub.

In her mind's eye, Regin threw her head back and let out a hoarse cry. In reality, she reached for the wall. It wasn't sturdy enough to hold her up. What she needed, what she craved, was to dig her nails into the strong chest of a dragon shifter.

"How was the hunt, sister?"

Regin straightened and turned. Her sister Siggy walked up the hall. Siggy's pale white hair was loose around her golden shoulders. Her bright eyes were full of mischief as usual. There was a hint of sympathy as they trained on Regin.

"That bad?" Siggy turned her around. "You don't look bloody."

"I'm not," said Regin "It wasn't. Everything went fine. I'm just overheated is all."

"But your eyes are glazed. Your tits are tight. And

your skin is flushed." Siggy lifted an eyebrow. "If I didn't know any better, I'd say you looked aroused."

Siggy started chuckling at the unlikely notion of Regin's arousal. But the thing about laughing at someone else's expense was that an inhalation was necessary to get the sound of mirth out of the throat. That deep breath, coupled with what Siggy saw with her own eyes, must have solidified the conclusion.

"You little slut!"

Had that slur come from any of her other sisters, it would be a bad thing. A very bad thing. Valkyrie were the immaculate creation of the Goddess. Crafted with the distilled essence of their ethereal father. Incubated in the thigh of their Mother, because She had better things to do with Her toned belly. And cut out of Her calf, because the hell would She push out a being from Her vagina like an animal.

The point being, the daughters of the Goddess were purebred, unvarnished, unsoiled and unsullied creations. They did not think about, pine for, nor do coitus. Except Siggy.

"Who?" Siggy demanded, her golden eyes glowing supernova bright. "Who popped your cherry? Was it Thor? Loki?"

Regin winced at the names of the male gods of

the realm. She didn't fail to note that her sister didn't bother naming any of the creatures a peg down from the gods, like the wolves, or the bears, or the lions... or dragons.

"But both Thor and Loki are in Jotunheim battling Frost Giants." Siggy looked from her sister and the great door to Valhalla. Then back to her sister. Her nose wrinkled. "Did you do it with a human?"

"Ew, Siggy." Regin had to swallow hard to keep the bile in her stomach. But at least her nipples relaxed at the gross inquiry.

Siggy threw up her hands. "No judgment here, sis. You know what they say about the bad guys."

Regin did not want to know what they said about bad guys. She would never let a human anywhere near her private, pink spots. The mere thought was disgusting.

"Listen, honey, you do what and who you want on your time," said Siggy. "Just don't let Hilda find out. You know how she is."

Regin did know how her eldest sister was. Hilda had had a thing for Thor since the two were made conscious. Thor considered Hilda the best warrior he knew, aside from himself. He considered her the smartest battle strategist, beside himself. He even considered her the best of friends. But that was it. It was clear he harbored no other emotion for the first-born of the Valkyrie.

Thor had no clue that Hilda harbored any feelings for him. And since she couldn't get what she wanted from the god she wanted, Hilda had long ago cockblocked all her other sisters from having a taste of any male species.

"Whoever he is, he's clearly on your mind," Siggy was saying. "Just go diddle him and be done. An orgasm can be very centering."

Diddle him? And be done? Could it really be that simple? Could she simply scratch this itch the one time and not think about it again?

CHAPTER 4

The pitiful sounds of a woman's wails greeted Draco when he closed the door of the castle behind him. She'd been sobbing when he'd left. She should be hoarse by now, but her cries continued.

The guilt-wracked over him as it had the last two times this had happened. He flexed his fingers. His palms itched to reach for the door handle. To run back out. To seek out the arms of a woman, any woman, to lose himself in for a few brief moments of mindlessness.

Only now there was a new problem. His mind had not stopped thinking of the Valkyrie and her sweet heat as she crouched over top of him. Even now, his dick was hard from the touch of her breath on his lips. His mouth watered thinking about those tight little buds that he knew would've pressed against her armor. His balls tightened at the memory of being right up under her warm core.

A door slammed opened. Then thundered shut. A roar shook the bricks of the castle. Followed by the wet sound of claws digging into flesh. And then finally, another feminine wail.

Draco didn't know which way to turn? He couldn't go out the door to seek the Valkyrie. If he dared entered Asgard and stated his intentions he'd be thrown into the Halls of Valhalla.

Running up those stairs to assist the woman in need would do neither of them any good. In fact, he knew he would likely have claws sunk into his flesh if he dared interfere with the claiming ritual. He'd learned that the first time he'd gotten between his father and one of his brothers. Both males were now dead.

"She's mine," growled his brother Drogo. He ducked a punch and then went for the legs of the male that blocked his path.

"I'm next in line," shouted their eldest brother Drek. He jumped, wings flapping to avoid Drogo's strike. "By right she's mine."

"You'll have to fight me for her."

"Isn't that what we're doing?"

The two brothers faced off. Both were in states of half shift. Drek had his wings out. Drogo had his claws out. They were both naked. Gashes and open wounds were etched on their flesh like tribal markings.

This was how Draco had left them. Fighting for the latest human sacrifice to arrive in the Veil. Their father had fought to the death for the last one and lost. Before that, his father had killed his eldest son for the right to claim a different human female who had arrived on their doorstep.

This one had been left in the Mosaic Mountains and sold to the highest bidder. Drogo and Drek had teamed up, putting together their silver and gold to pay off the human males who had delivered the sacrifice. They'd won her from the others. But now one of them had to win the right to claim the wailing woman.

Draco hated the barbaric practice. But it was the way of the realm, the way of their kind since the Goddess who'd created them had not seen fit to craft female dragon shifters. She left the dragons with no other choice than to turn to human females and the greedy human males who coveted the precious stones in the dragons' mountains.

The problem was, over the centuries those sacrifices were coming less and less. The dragons didn't know why. They didn't care about the reason. All they cared about was claiming one of the women for their own regardless of who they had to kill to do it.

Draco sighed as he leaned against the door. Unfortunately, he was too loud with his sound of disdain. His brothers' gazes whipped around to him.

Draco held up his hands. "I have no claim in this fight. I make no offer for the woman."

"Fool," spat Drogo.

"Coward," hissed Drek.

"Go hide between a fairy's thighs and leave us be."

Draco pointed up. "If it's just the same to you, I'm going to go to my room and sleep."

As he stepped forward, his brothers tracked his every move. They balanced on their toes ready to strike if he got too near the room where the female had locked herself in. The lock was a moot point. Any dragon could bust the door down. His brothers would once this battle was done and one of them was likely dead.

Draco made a wide circuit around his brothers to

get to his room on the third floor. He would've flown, but he didn't trust his dragon enough. One strong whiff of the human female and the beast might decide it wanted a taste.

Not likely, though. The only thing his tongue hungered for, the very reason his stomach rumbled, the cause for his dripping incisors was for a female he couldn't possibly, ever, in a million years, hope to taste.

It was insanity to want a Valkyrie.

Still, he couldn't help wonder that if he was mad for wanting her then wasn't she also a bit touched too? He hadn't imagined that her nostrils had flared when she felt his manhood against her covered sex. He hadn't made up that glance she stole when her golden eyes dipped to his lips. He hadn't fabricated the reality that her hips had swiveled once, almost twice, when she'd crouched overtop of him.

But was he imagining that she was sitting on his windowsill staring up at the moon?

Draco blinked. He rubbed his eyes. Then he blinked again.

She was still there. Dressed not in the pale blue battle armor of her kind. She wore a simple white shift that was near translucent in the moon's light. Her golden hair was down around her shoulders. It hung in lush waves that touched the small of her back. Her arms were bare, except for the daggers strapped around each of her biceps. Her feet were encased in black, heeled boots that reached up to cover her knees. Draco suspected there would be daggers in each one as well.

He should be alarmed. He should be frightened. Instead, he was utterly and completely turned on.

"Hello," he said.

Her beautiful face swiveled to face him. Her beauty stole his breath. High cheekbones. Heart-shaped lips. Wide, soulful eyes he felt himself getting lost in.

And then she was a blur.

In the space of a breath, she was on him. Dagger brandished, pointy end at his neck. He felt the trickle of his blood meander down his throat all the way to his beating heart.

"Hello," she said. Her tone was polite, proper even. Which belied the next words that came out of her mouth. "I'm here because I want you to fuck me."

Part Two of *The Valkyrie's Claim* will be in your inbox in just a week!
While you wait, you might want to check out the next book in the Last Dragons Series.
The Dragon's Ambivalent Sacrifice is available now exclusively on Amazon and Kindle Unlimited.

Grab your copy today!

CHAPTER 5

Velvet. That was what his flesh felt like under Regin's palm. Firm velvet that she wanted to roll her body around in.

She had seen Draco practically naked earlier this evening. That memory of him did not do his body justice. The male was a beautiful specimen of her Mother's craftsmanship.

Even, honey-gold skin like the finest of gemstones. Valkyrie were attracted to fine, shiny things. Regin wanted to wrap Draco's body around hers like a necklace and wear him.

She had been restless all night back in the hall with her sisters. She'd downed goblet after goblet of ale, but her body was a tight coil of need. Every time she'd closed her eyes, she saw Draco's tight ass clenching and releasing. Every time she opened her eyes, she remembered his long, slick member playing hide and seek in the moon's pale light. Now it was within her grasp.

Flying across the realms and landing at his castle in the dead of night had been the best decision she had made in centuries. Just the scent of him cooled her overheated flesh. Draco smelled of burnt wood, warm earth and some spicy scent she couldn't identify.

All of her pink bits tightened. Her nipples pebbled like a precious stone. Her mouth watered as though she were glimpsing his horde of treasure. The space between her legs throbbed as though a dragon was taking a pickax to it in search of hidden gems.

Well, this dragon certainly could take his ax to her center. Hilda often said that their Mother gave them ten fingers for a reason. But Regin had never found feminine release on her own.

She was prepared to let Draco mine her secret depths to get to her precious jewels. In him, she was certain she'd find the relief she sought. And, after his earlier performance, she was even more certain that he knew what to do to bring her satisfaction.

"I'm sorry," the sexy dragon said. "What did you say?"

They had been staring at each other in total silence for Goddess knew how long. It took Regin a moment to respond to him. She liked the way his voice rumbled through her eardrums.

"I said I want you to fuck me."

That was the right word. She'd heard males use it enough. Heck, her sister Kára used the word as a comma whenever she spoke.

"I can be clearer," she said. "I want you to take your cock, preferably when it's stiff and engorged, and place it inside my vagina. From what I under-stand, it's best to do that when my folds are slick. Then I want you to thrust repeatedly until you bring me to my feminine release. I believe it's called an orgasm."

"I…"

Draco cleared his throat. But he was still having trouble forcing words out. It might have something to do with the blade that was against his neck.

Regin removed the blade. A bead of dark red blood pooled at the place she'd pricked. The tiny bead shimmered in the light of the room, like a ruby.

Regin's eyes glittered gold. Rubies were her favorites. Next to emeralds and topaz. Who was she kidding? Like all Valkyrie, there wasn't a gem she met that didn't dazzle her.

The sanguine bead of blood made her incisors water. She wanted to lick it. To bite him. To mark his flesh.

"I'm afraid I'll have to decline."

Regin cocked her head to the side. Did he say decline? Was that some sexual position she didn't know?

He couldn't mean he was turning her down. For sex. He was a man.

"You don't want me?" she asked.

"I didn't say that."

Regin reached to her forearm holster and brandished her other blade. "Speak plainly, scaly boy."

Draco gulped and stepped back. His spicy scent overwhelmed her nostrils. But it wasn't a tinge of fear she smelled. That scent she knew too well from her captures all these years.

"You are a daughter of the Goddess," said the dragon. "To even touch you, I'm sure would be sacrilege."

"I'm a grown woman."

"Trust me." Draco's gaze roamed the length of her. "I can see that."

Regin resheathed her daggers. She grabbed the

hem of her nightgown and unsheathed her body so that he could have a better look. "I just want you to see what I'm offering you before you lock onto this stupid decision."

Draco groaned like a man in pure agony. He squeezed his eyes shut. Only for a second before wrenching them back open and staring. Then he shut them again and groaned.

"Am I not pleasing to your eyes?" Regin asked.

"Goddess have mercy." His eyes were open. Wide-open. Taking in every curve of her form.

"I scent your arousal, dragon. I can see that your member is stiff."

Draco's hand went to his groin area. His breathing was becoming labored. His gaze was latched on her breasts.

"My form is pleasing to you." Regin ticked off the evidence with her fingers. "Your cock stands at the ready. It doesn't appear that it would be any trouble to-"

Before she could come to the inevitable conclusion of her argument, her feet were off the floor. Her body was in the air. Her back was slammed against the door. Draco had her thighs parted and his body between them.

It didn't occur to Regin until later that this might

have been a move of seduction. She was a warrior. So obviously she saw the move as one of aggression.

She dug her heel into the sensitive spot behind his knee. Draco dropped like a stone and she was on him, over him. Two blades were at his throat and more ruby red blood trickled down his throat begging her to taste.

CHAPTER 6

Once again, Draco landed flat on his ass with a killer brandishing steel at his throat. Unfortunately, the blow to his head did not knock a single ounce of sense into his thick, reptilian skull.

Draco hated violence. He avoided fights like they were the plague. But something about this woman and her blades kept his dick hard.

Fairies were lithe, willowy creatures. They weren't flab, but none had muscles on their arms and legs. Regin's muscles weren't large, but they were powerful enough to take a full-grown dragon down.

Her perky breasts swayed over him, just behind the sharp blades at his neck. If he lifted his head he could capture one of her pink nipples in his mouth.

True, he'd also wind up decapitated himself. He was busy debating if it would be worth a taste.

"Did I misread your signals?" The Valkyrie asked in that polite tone. Say what you want about the Goddess or Her daughters, or the wayward All-Father, but at least this godling had some manners. "Were you trying to seduce me when you slammed my body against the door and pressed yourself between my thighs?"

"Ummm." Draco gulped, then spat out the truth. "Yes."

"Oh."

Regin retracted the blades and sat back on her haunches. Her bare core planted down on his belly.

Draco held still, though everything in him urged him to wiggle his hips until she was just an inch lower and sitting right on his cock.

"Does that mean you agree to my request?" she asked. "Will you fuck me?"

He sat up. They both gasped as her body slid down, right where he wanted it. It was as though they snapped into place, a key fitting into a lock it never knew it was meant for.

Regin still held blades in both of her hands. From his vantage point, Draco saw the glint of silver steel peeking out of her boot. Even without the blades, he knew she could tear him in two.

None of that mattered. He had her exactly where he wanted her; right in his lap. His cock throbbed so hard Draco was certain it would punch through the layer of fabric between them.

Soon, he soothed the savage beast. He could have her soon.

Draco leaned into Regin. The first brush of his lips against hers was a hard strike of flint. Being that he was a fire-breathing dragon, that mere taste nearly consumed him.

Regin leaned away. "What are you doing?"

"Kissing you."

Her brow furrowed. "Why?"

"Because I want to know what you taste like."

Her gaze widened. "You want to eat me?"

Draco's lips split into a devilish grin. "For starters."

Regin's hand came to his neck. At least this time it was just her strong fingers around his throat and not a blade.

"Don't worry," he said. "I won't use my teeth. Just my tongue. I want to taste your mouth, your breasts, your core."

Regin's tone was uncertain when she spoke. "But I want your cock, not your tongue."

Draco licked at his lower lip. "I'd like to give you both, if I may."

The Valkyrie still looked doubtful.

He rose with her in his arms. She stiffened. But she let him carry her to his bed.

Draco lay his predator down on her back. He ran his hands along her strong flesh. Regin shivered under his touch.

He came over her and pressed his mouth to hers. She opened to him. She was awkward at first, but soon she was pressing into his mouth. Tasting, sipping, nibbling.

And then she flipped him so that she was on top and looming over him.

"Sorry," she said. "I'm not a submissive woman."

"I don't mind at all."

She kissed him again, deeper, longer until they both were breathless.

Draco lay back on the bed, scooting until his head met the headboard. Looking back at Regin, he crooked a finger at her. "Come here. I want you to sit on my face."

"You want me to smother you?"

"Something like that. I told you, I want to taste you."

"I told you, I want to sit on your cock."

"Let me prepare your passage to take me."

Regin looked down. His straining cock was clear to make out. It had raised a tent city in his pants. "Yes, you are a Big Daddy aren't you."

Draco blinked. What had she just called him?

"Very well." She brought her thighs to either side of his head. "How will you -ohhh."

He latched onto her nub with no preamble. Her hips raised, fluttering like a bird on its first flight. After a few of his suckles, Regin came in for a landing. As he licked from her nub to her entrance, she crashed into him.

CHAPTER 7

Regin had no idea her body could do that. Boil up like a volcano and explode. Tremors wracked her body. And they hadn't done the actual fucking yet.

Draco brought her down so that her hips settled over his. The core of her still throbbed with aftershocks when she sat down on his hard rod. For a moment, she wasn't sure if she could take more. She quickly tossed that worry away.

She wanted all of him; every bit he had to offer. And boy oh boy was there a hefty offering waiting between her thighs.

Regin lifted her hips, sliding her entrance over the thick head of his cock.

Draco's large hands came onto either side of her hips and halted her downward progress.

Regin flashed her eyes at him. She knew that technically the cock was his and she had asked to play with it. Sharing in her world, which was filled with powerful, unflinching women, amounted to taking what one wanted and asking for forgiveness later, or fighting it out. Regin was prepared to fight the dragon to get his member inside her.

"Are you denying me, dragon?"

"No..." Draco's grin was sheepish, embarrassed.

Before that moment, Regin had only seen him as a tool for her use. But with that self-deprecating smile, something shifted inside of her. She saw him as... well, a person.

Draco was laid out beneath her like an offering. His chest was a sculpted mass of twin peaks. His abdomen was a valley of ridges and ripples. At some point while or after he was licking her, he'd divested himself of his pants. Dark hair curled around a massive erection that should have given Regin pause. Problem was she didn't want to pause.

"It's just..." His hand reached up to her face.

Regin flinched, but she didn't move beyond his reach. His fingers brushed her cheeks in a soft caress. It was almost reverent.

"Forgive me," he whispered, "but I don't know your name."

"My name?"

"I'd like to know whose name to scream when I'm in the throes of passion." He grinned again, the devil returning to the spark in his green eyes, showing that his beast was near the surface.

His words took Regin aback. She knew that men enjoyed the sexual act -often more than the women they were partnered with. There was no dispute that Draco had pleasured her senseless with that one act. It had never occurred to her that she could give a man pleasure.

"Regin. My name is Regin."

Draco repeated her name. He trilled the R and softened the G. The sound of her name on his lips brought pleasure. The man was truly gifted.

Her gaze slipped to his neck. Again, her incisors watered. The urge to bite, to mark, to claim came over her. That trance was broken when she felt the head of his cock breach her tight sheath.

Regin gasped. Her claws dug into the flesh of his chest. Her thighs trembled at the invasion. Instead of taking it slow, she was eager to march full speed ahead like the warrior she was. And so Regin pushed her hips down. Instead of pleasure, she met with resistance and pain.

"Easy there, love." Draco lifted her hips, but he

did not lift her off him. "Let's take it easy. Inch by inch."

"You have a lot of inches."

There it was again, that impish grin. "I intend to give you every last one. But in due time."

He reached for her face again. This time he cupped her chin in his hand. His fiery gaze was on her lips.

"May I kiss you again, Regin?"

She liked that he asked. He had her in a vulnerable position. Naked, splayed over him. And yet he asked her permission.

Regin nodded. She leaned in to reach his lips. But Draco had already ducked his head. His tongue met the nipple of her right breast.

Regin arched her back at the sensation. The move brought her breasts deeper into Draco's mouth. It also dropped her hips down another inch on his stiff rod. The triple sensation sent an explosion of seismic proportions through her body and her core clenched.

This time, the clenching happened around a stiff rod and not an empty channel. Her body behaved like a siphon, sucking him deeper into her channel. The way became easy as her intimate wetness filled up between the two of them.

As the orgasm raged on, her intimate passage continued its suction until she was fully seated on his erection. All the while Draco murmured around her breasts.

"By the Goddess, you're the sweetest thing I've ever tasted."

"You're like velvet in my hands, love."

"Never wanted anything so much."

"That's it, love. Take it. Take all of me."

It was that last plea that made her do it. Her mind was a haze from the strength of the orgasm. She threw back her head, her incisors sharp. Then struck, biting down on his neck.

Draco's growl reverberated through her body, coaxing another orgasm. She felt his body tremble inside hers. His hard cock grew thicker. She was being filled with a warm wetness.

When he pulled back to look at her he looked dazed. Blood trickled down from his shoulder. She tasted the metallic tint of it on her tongue.

She knew she should be ashamed at what she'd done. But all that came over her was a feeling of rightness. All that kept going through her head was the single word...

Mine.

CHAPTER 8

Chapter Eight

Draco had had a lot of sex in his life. He'd fucked in every position known to man and beast. He'd screwed in every location imaginable. But he'd never once lost control of his body during his randy sessions.

He'd had some powerful orgasms in his life. Spasms that made his toes curl, his balls deplete, and his eyes roll back. All those were a pale comparison to what he was feeling now.

Every nerve ending in his body had exploded. He was left in tatters on the bed. Not a single piece of himself was recognizable. But that wasn't the mind-blowing part.

As the shakes and shivers of his orgasm died down, he was left feeling utterly content.

There was no emptiness that needed filling. No anxiety to find someone else with whom to do it again. As he sat on his bed, holding Regin to him, he felt entirely at peace.

His dick was still hard, eager for round two. But he knew he needed to back off. She'd been a virgin only a few minutes ago. She'd be sore. And besides, he wasn't sure she wanted another go with him.

Her curiosity was settled now. She'd had sex. Mind-blowing, amazing, life-changing sex. She might not care to repeat the experience ever again. Which would be a travesty to Draco, as he only wanted a repeat performance with her. In fact, he couldn't even fathom performing with another female again.

Regin's breathing was ragged now. Perhaps she hadn't had the same mind-blowing experience? Perhaps she was in pain? Few women found their first times to be pleasurable.

Draco pulled away to search out her face. What he found when he looked at her was blood. "I've hurt you?"

"No." Her brow crinkled. Her throat worked. "I've hurt you."

What was she talking about? She had made him feel amazing, whole, complete. Her gaze was settled on his neck. That's when he felt it.

Vaguely in his mind, he registered that there had been a pinch on his shoulder. But the pleasure of his climax had been so intense that he hadn't thought twice about any pain. Now, seeing the blood on Regin's face and feeling the twin punctures on his shoulder, the bloody realization dawned on him.

"You bit me?"

She nodded.

"You marked me?"

"I... I'm... I..."

It looked as though she was trying to say that she was sorry. But her mouth couldn't form the words. Or wouldn't.

"I did," she said finally. "I bit you." She swallowed hard and lifted her chin.

It was an adorable move. Draco would've been utterly charmed by it. Except... what did this mean?

"Did I hurt you very much?" she asked.

There was no pain. The spot tingled, like a fizzy drink he'd once tried from beyond the Veil.

Regin's eyes kept darting from the bite mark on

his neck to his lips, his eyes, and back. He couldn't quite read her expression.

Was that remorse? Maybe guilt? Definitely a touch of defiance. She was a Valkyrie after all.

"Why did you bite me?" Draco asked.

"I don't know?" For the first time they'd met, likely the first time in her life, she looked vulnerable.

Regin looked him straight in the eyes. He wasn't sure what she was searching for. She need only ask and he'd give it to her, whatever it was.

"That's not entirely true," she said after a long moment.

Draco waited. She was still in his lap. He was still inside of her, though he had softened. He knew he should lift her off him. The longer they stayed like this, the sorer she'd be for it. But he couldn't bring himself to part from her.

"Something inside me..." She began and stopped. "You'll think me touched in the head."

"No." He pulled her closer, fitting her more snuggly on his semi erection, wrapping his arms tightly around her.

Regin came without protest. Her hands rested on his chest. Her gaze locked with his. There it was again, something he never thought he'd see in his lifetime. He was seeing it twice in one night. Vulnerability within a Valkyrie.

"A voice inside my head told me to do it," she said. "It insisted you were mine."

Draco had known the words to be true before Regin said them aloud. He'd felt the same pull to her. But he hadn't dared voice them. She was far braver than he.

"When a dragon takes a sacrifice," he said, "he marks her to warn off others."

Regin's eyes flashed golden with a warning. "I don't want anyone touching you again. You are mine."

She was right. She was touched in the head. This was insane.

And Draco was entirely on board with the insanity.

"After a dragon marks his sacrifice," he continued, "he claims her by-"

"Fucking?" she said. "Looks like I did it out of order. Does it still count?"

He couldn't form words. He was so captivated. He'd been captured and marked and mated by a Valkyrie. He nodded.

"So, I've claimed you," she said. "You belong to me now."

This could never work. Dragons did the claiming. Valkyrie didn't do males. But the hell was he giving her up.

"Yes, love," he said. "Yes, I do."

"No more fairies."

"What's a fairy?"

She grinned. She leaned in, her lips seeking his. But before they could seal this crazy deal, a scream tore through the castle.

Regin was out of his lap and crouched in a fighting stance before he blinked.

"Who was that?" she demanded.

"Oh, that? Just the resident human sacrifice."

Golden eyes blazed at him, along with the glint of her dagger. Instead of fear, Draco was once again turned on. But he'd have to do some sweet talking quick because his new mistress had her ire and her dagger aimed at his jewels.

"You took a sacrifice?"

Part Three of *The Valkyrie's Claim* will be in your inbox in just a week!

While you wait, you might want to check out the next book in the Last Dragons Series.
The Dragon's Ambivalent Sacrifice is available now exclusively on Amazon and Kindle Unlimited.

Grab your copy today!

CHAPTER 9

Every day after wrangling with human miscreants, or battling with Frost Giants, or fighting with her sisters, Regin always felt a soreness in her body. The aches and pains were a necessary annoyance in her line of work. And the sensations never lasted long.

The soreness Regin felt in her body after Draco worked her over couldn't be described as anything except delicious. The ache between her thighs was a welcome delight. The pain in her channel where he'd breached her virgin skin was a distant memory that she wanted to pull back and experience again and again.

Sex was a battlefield she would throw herself on the sword for. Again. And again. But the battlecry that just sounded outside of their love nest put her on high alert.

Regin rolled off her lover and brandished her weapons. Crouching in front of her new possession, the dragon known as Draco, she was at the ready to protect what was hers.

"What was that?" Regin demanded.

Draco tensed, but only in his brows. His body remained relaxed and languid on the bed. His cock rested on his belly, the single eye weeping its satiation.

"Oh, that? Just the resident human sacrifice."

Sacrifice? Had she heard him right? He'd taken a sacrifice?

Regin left her defensive post and pounced back on the bed. She crouched over Draco, her daggers aimed at the crown jewel of his person. "You took a sacrifice?"

Could she have been so naive? He'd had a fairy earlier in the night. Was she a fool to believe that he might feel something for her so quickly, that she might be special, different from all the others? All the while he was coveting a human breeder down the hall.

Draco held up his hands. His gaze never left hers. His voice was quiet but stern as he spoke. "I did not. She belongs to my brothers. One of them. I'm not sure which? Whichever is still alive on the other side of the door."

Regin looked back to the door as though she could see through it and see the dueling dragons on the other side. She turned back to Draco. Her head tilted inquisitively. "Did your brothers best you for her?"

Draco blinked as though he didn't understand.

"Would you like me to go out and win her for you?" asked Regin.

"Win her for me?" Draco parroted.

Regin hopped off the bed and started for the door. No way would she let any other males take a prize from her dragon. She'd slay both his brothers and bring her man back the breeder.

For show. Not for anything else. The female would definitely not be having sex with her dragon. Draco was hers.

Before Regin could turn the knob, Draco placed himself between her and the door.

"No," he said.

"No?" she asked.

"No," he repeated. "I don't want you to go out and win her for me. I don't want her. I want you."

Regin's lips formed a perfect O shape, but no

sound passed her mouth. She lowered her daggers, standing unguarded before her dragon. "You do?"

Draco's hand cupped her face. "I do."

He brushed his thumb over her lower lip. Regin had the instinct to nip him. But she didn't. She suspected this was one of those tender moments, one where a woman should be pliant.

So she dropped her weapons and leaped on him. With her bare feet, she wrapped her thighs around his waist. Yanking his head back with her hands, she plundered his mouth with her tongue.

In response, Draco chuckled in delight as he kneaded her bare bottom.

They were almost to the bed when another agonizing wail shook the rafters. Draco lowered his head to her shoulder and sighed.

Regin did not like the heaviness that settled along his brow. She unwound herself from his waist and pulled on her dress and boots.

"What are you doing?" he asked.

"I'm going to check on the situation."

"No, Regin. It's best if we don't get involved."

But she had already wrenched the door open and was walking into the hall. The scene she came upon made her want to retch. Regin was made of strong stuff, she was a warrior, a daughter of the Goddess, but even she had to turn away from the scene before her. When she did, she was met with the soft cushion of Draco's embrace.

CHAPTER 10

They were dead.

Draco hadn't truly expected a different outcome. He had expected one of them to live. But they both were dead.

Drogo's body lay at an odd angle on the stair. He hadn't fallen down the staircase. His head was still at the top. His legs were hanging off the rails. His torso was at a right angle between the other pieces.

Drek was lying face down in the hall. His body was unmoving. His body was also facing up. His chest was to the ceiling.

In the battle to claim one woman, both males had lost their lives.

Draco cradled Regin in his arms, shielding her from the madness that was the lives of the dragons.

He was now the last of his weyr. There were very few dragons left. Only one family of males remained, led by a vicious patriarch that had slain many of his kind to win three sacrifices. Unfortunately, Gneiss had six surviving sons, so this madness would likely continue for another generation. Unless those males killed one another as well and the dragons were no more.

A wailing cry broke Draco's solemn reverie. The miserable moan lifted Regin's head from his chest. It was the female sacrifice.

"I suppose she's yours now," said Regin.

Draco looked down into the Valkyrie's face. Her perfectly heart-shaped face. Her pinched lips. Her wide eyes.

"I don't want her," he said. "I love you."

Regin's eyes widened further. They flashed a gold so bright that Draco had to squint as he looked into her gaze.

"Love?" she said. "You love me?"

"I'm sure it's insane." He brushed at the corner of her eyelid, trying to touch the light of the ray.

"It's madness," she whispered.

"A dragon and a Valkyrie." He chided, waiting for her to put the notion down, slash it with her blades.

"I feel it too," she said.

Her words might as well have broken his heart open. His breath of relief was the pouring out of his beating heart.

"Then we're both mad," he said.

They were. A pairing like this had never happened in the Veil. It was not meant to be.

But here they were.

Draco couldn't remember his life before Regin put a dagger to his throat. He couldn't fathom an existence without her nails digging into his skin. Her body over him, demanding satisfaction.

As he gazed down at her, the reflection of love in her bright eyes dimmed. Her bright features darkened, like an unwelcome cloud come to rain on their picnic.

"Mother didn't make me for breeding," she said.

Breeding? Children? Draco shook his head. "I never wanted to bring a child into this world."

Regin eyed him skeptically. There were two dead bodies on the ground who had fought for the privilege of siring more of his kind.

"Whatever your Mother may have made me for, I reject Her plan now."

A tiny gasp escaped his Valkyrie's lips.

"Whatever She made you for, you can make a

different choice," he said. "Choose me as I choose you."

Slowly, a wicked grin spread across Regin's lovely features. Draco spied the mischief dawning in his new mate. Because that's what she was; his mate.

In bed.

In life.

In love.

"Yes," she said. "I choose you."

Draco tilted her head back and claimed her mouth. Regin dug her nails into the back of his neck and pulled him closer. He didn't mind that his fierce warrior took control. Not so long as she let him have his way with her.

And she did now.

Mostly.

Their lips tangled. Their tongues tussled. Their incisors tore.

Draco tasted blood as he gulped down the fiery taste of his mate. Regin was insatiable as she sucked at his top lip, the edge of his bottom lip, the underside of his tongue. His Valkyrie was a fast learner and she was quickly mastering her lessons. Draco was more than happy to submit.

"Excuse me?"

Draco and Regin broke apart. Standing in the

open doorway of the once locked bedroom was a small human woman. Her hair was flaming red. She wore a shift with a design of pale colors splashed on the fabric. A circle with three prongs in the center was over her chest with the letters PEACE in black. Her long legs were encased in dark blue fabric that flared out over her feet.

"I think I took some really bad acid," she said, holding her hand to her head. "I wanna go home now. Can one of you give me a ride?"

CHAPTER 11

Regin did not understand the draw of human females. They were soft. Weak. Breakable. And easily exhausted.

"Can we stop for a second?" said the female. "I'm not feeling so well."

"Again?" grumbled Regin.

"I don't do well with heights."

Regin's dragon soared through the night's sky with her and the human on it's back. There were no clouds or rain. It was a peaceful ride high above the treetops.

Still, the human female clutched to Regin's middle like she was in danger of falling off. It was another reason Regin didn't understand humans.

They rode horses sitting upon saddles. They drove in the metal boxcars with a woven strap over their bodies. It made no sense to Regin.

"We're nearly there," Regin insisted.

Up ahead were the Mountains of Gaia. The range was the closest break in the Veil. It was also near the mines of the last weyr of dragons, the patriarch of which was a particularly unpleasant male. Thoughts of Gneiss left Regin's mind when she saw Draco flying beside her dragon.

The male was magnificent even in dragon form. After they disposed of the human female, Regin had plans to ride Draco again. First in dragon form on his back. Then in man form on his front.

"Oh god, I'm going to barf."

The sound of the human being sick behind her brought Regin back to the present and the task at hand. The sooner she got rid of the chit the sooner she could get on with the rest of her night and the rest of her life.

With a dragon.

Regin wasn't sure how it would work between her and Draco? Males were not welcome in Valhalla. Unless they were captives. Or if they were Thor. She doubted her sisters would overlook a big dragon walking into the halls for dinner. Especially not Hilda.

Perhaps she and Draco could keep to his castle. He was the last of the Tormaline dragons. There would be no one to contest that decision.

But was that too soon? To move in together? They'd known each other for less than a day.

Draco landed first at the base of the mountain. His long neck turned right and left, searching for danger. It was adorable. He was trying to protect her.

Regin knew her sisters had her back when they were in battle. But none had ever needed to come to her assistance before. They were all Valkyrie.

The human female climbed off the back of the dragon and retched in the grass. The flowers moved their bulbs out of the way but still got splattered with her regurgitated meal.

"I'm usually not this bad with flying," said the female. "But I usually fly inside a plane and not on a dragon. Man, I am so high."

Regin had seen the metal tubes humans flew in. They were Coca Cola bottles without wings. They could fall from the sky and break at any moment.

"I'll take her through and be right back," Regin said to Draco.

He stood naked, having shifted back into his human form. Regin took a moment to admire what was now and would forever be hers. She intended to toss the woman through the Veil and hurry back for her rides with her beast of a man.

"What do we have here?" came a deep, gravely voice.

Draco pushed Regin behind him and faced off against the old dragon who lorded these mountains. Regin took a moment to admire her dragon's strong back muscles before she turned her attention to Gneiss.

"A new sacrifice?" The old dragon licked his incisors.

"She's not for you," said Draco.

"I know," said Gneiss. "I fought for her and lost to your brothers." The dragon's cuts and bruises were still visible. "And now it appears I'll get a second chance since you don't fight for women."

The female whimpered behind Regin and Draco. Regin tried to hide her disgust at the woman. The human was a discredit to her gender. Regin had never whimpered a day in her life.

Well, not in fear. She had whimpered at the pleasure Draco unleashed on her body. Watching him puff out his chest against the elder dragon was having the same effect. Regin felt a whimper of lust rise in her throat.

"She's mine now," said Draco. "And I'm returning her back to her world."

Gneiss roared a chuckle. Behind the dragon, Regin saw a small boy poke his head from behind a rock. The boy's eyes flashed blue, but not at Regin and Draco. The baby dragon's eyes flashed at his father.

It must be one of Gneiss' sons. Regin had heard the whelps were a different breed from their sire. Her sister Morrigan told that the boys cared for one of the sacrifices who survived, but not with her mental faculties intact. If this blue-eyed whelp was any indication, Regin believed the story to be true.

Gneiss leaped. He left the ground as a male and partially shifted into dragon. His talons were aimed right for the female.

Before Regin had a moment to react, Draco leaped into the air to meet the dragon. It had been told across the Veil that Draco was a lover and not a fighter. That statement was proven wrong as her beautiful dragon delivered blow after blow to Gneiss without shifting a single scale.

Regin rocked back on her heels and watched as her lover punched, kicked, and pummeled the larger dragon into the earth. It was both beautiful and arousing to watch. As Gneiss fell to the ground in defeat, the blue-eyed whelp grinned a toothsome grin before disappearing into the shadows.

"You were magnificent," Regin said as Draco came towards her.

"He was," came a breathy voice behind her.

Regin craned her neck to see the human woman no longer whimpering. She had an appreciative grin on her face and she was eyeing Draco's package. Before Regin could pluck out the woman's eyeballs, Draco settled a hand on her nape.

"Take her through before we have to deal with any of Gneiss' sons," said Draco. "I've known them all to be level headed, but you never know when a dragon catches a whiff of human female."

"But not you?" asked Regin.

"No." He brushed a stray strand of her hair behind her ear. "I've acquired a solitary taste for Valkyrie."

Draco planted a kiss on her lips. Regin leaned in to gather more of his taste, but he pulled back.

"Hurry through," he said when he let her up. "I shouldn't be so close to the Veil. We don't want any of your sisters to learn of this."

Regin cuffed the human female by her upper

arm and marched her to the Veil. The female went without protest, though her eyes lingered on Draco as she walked away.

Once on the other side, the human took a deep breath and fell to her knees. "I'm starting to think I'm not high anymore."

Regin rolled her eyes. They were at the base of a new mountain. In the distance, she read a sign that said Hollywood.

"Go on about your life," said Regin. "You're lucky those dragons died before they touched you."

"Oh," the female grinned. "They touched me, all right."

"They?" asked Regin. "Both of them.

"Yeah. And? It's the 1960's. I'm a sexually liberated woman."

The free woman came to standing and stretched her body, her small breasts arched in the light of the bright sign. Then she doubled over again, holding her stomach.

"Oh god. I'm going to be sick again."

Regin shook her head at the woman. She didn't have time for this. She had a dragon to get back to and ride. She turned her back and headed through the Veil.

If the woman was pregnant the dragons wouldn't

survive in this realm. It wasn't her problem any longer. She was going to claim her prize.

"There you are, sister." Hilda stood with her sword at Draco's throat. "Look what we found trying to escape."

CHAPTER 12

For the third time this night, Draco found himself at the mercy of a woman with a blade to his neck. Only this time he wasn't turned on.

He'd avoided the Valkyrie Hilda all his life. Everyone knew she had a thing for the God of Thunder. Problem was the Thor only took notice of her battle prowess. That was probably why Hilda was the fiercest of all the Valkyrie. But, due to Thor's lack of acknowledgment, Hilda was also the biggest man-hater of them all.

Beside her were two other Valkyrie. The one Draco knew to be called Morrigan eyed the gem around his neck. The one he knew to be called Siggy eyed the package between his thighs.

He knew he should fear for his life. There was no

guarantee he would escape this latest scrap. Draco caught the scent of her before he saw her. In just a short amount of time, Regin had imprinted on his mind, his body, his soul. She came through the Veil swords blazing.

"Let him go, Hildy."

"Why would I do that, Reggie?" Hilda's frown was genuine. "He broke the rules. Dragons can't cross the Veil. What were you doing? Trying to steal a human sacrifice?"

"He wasn't breaking the rules," said Regin. "He was returning a sacrifice."

Hilda looked so confused that she dropped her blade from Draco's neck. "That's madness. A dragon would never release a human."

"He did." Regin didn't let loose her swords. She held them at the ready. "He didn't want her. He wanted me."

"You reptilian swine." Hilda's sword came back to Draco's neck. "You were trying to kill my sister?"

"He wasn't trying to kill me," Regin sighed. "He wants me as a man wants a woman."

Hilda frowned. Morrigan's lips twitched. Siggy clapped her hands.

"Oh, this is the one you were talking about?" Siggy eyed Draco appreciatively. "Nice one, sis."

"Do you mean he violated you?" asked Hilda.

"How was it?" asked Siggy.

"Did he give you any jewels?" asked Morrigan.

Regin ignored them all. Her focus was on the blade at Draco's throat. "Hilda, would you please remove the blade and give him back to me. He is mine."

"That's disgusting," said Hilda. "He's a male, a villain."

"He hasn't done anything I didn't ask him to do. In fact, I begged him to do most of it. He's one of the good ones."

"To take advantage of an innocent? He needs to taste my blade."

"He didn't break any laws. If you harm a hair on his head, so help me I'll shave off yours."

"Ohhh," chorused Morrigan and Siggy in the universal language of siblings egging each other on.

Draco knew Valkyrie were territorial, blood-thirsty creatures. But he wished the other two would shut it. Now really wasn't the time.

"Just because you're not getting any from the man you want doesn't mean we don't want any for ourselves," said Regin.

"Ohhh," winced Morrigan and Siggy.

Hilda's blade tensed.

Regin dug in her heels.

The two sisters stood for what seemed like hours, but the problem was only a few seconds. Finally, Hilda shoved Draco forward.

"You're a disappointment," Hilda spat. "Take your pet reptile, but don't think you'll bring him home."

"I'm moving out," said Regin. "Trust me, with our lovemaking you would ask me to leave soon or later."

Hilda made a face. Morrigan tilted her head. Siggy licked her lips.

"From this moment, the Veil is closed," Hilda announced to no one in particular. "No more sacrifices will be allowed in."

Though the pronouncement would not hurt him, Draco felt guilty for the six young dragons of these mountains. They would be the last of their kind. But perhaps it was for the best. At least the boys would have no reason to gut each other as they fought over human females.

Siggy came over and hugged Regin. She went to hug Draco, but Regin blocked her sister.

"Let me know if you need anything, sis," said Morrigan.

As a farewell, Hilda turned her back on her sister. Regin resheathed her weapons and turned to

Draco. As the two of them walked away from her family, Regin placed her hand in his.

"I know it's soon," she said, "since we've only known each other less than a day, but what do you think about me moving in for a while?"

Draco squeezed her hand. "How about forever? Is that long enough?"

Regin came into his embrace. She hugged him tightly, showing her strength. Even if she took his last breath he would go down with a smile for his Valkyrie.

"Is that vomit I smell?" he asked.

"Yes. That woman is probably pregnant. I doubt the whelps will survive on the other side. So it's nothing to worry about."

"What do we do now?"

"Well," Regin licked her lips. "I was hoping for a ride."

I hope you've enjoyed this prequel novella for the Last Dragons series.

Be sure and read each tale of those six young dragons to see how they gain sacrifices of their own and lose their hearts!

ABOUT INES JOHNSON

Lover of fairytales, folklore, and mythology, Ines Johnson spends her days reimagining the stories of old in a modern world. She writes books where damsels cause the distress, princesses wield swords, and moms save the world.

If you liked Ines' Vampires, then you'll love her Dragons; alpha male shifters, fated mates, and steamy romance with a touch of 80's nostalgia! To grab a free book from the world of the Last Dragons just visit https://ineswrites.com/ReaderGroup

MORE PARANORMAL ROMANCE BY INES JOHNSON

Dark Vintage
Her Vampire Prince
Her Vampire Lord
Her Vampire Knight
His Vampire Princess